My Phantom Lover

My Phantom Lover

Carol J. Aken

iUniverse, Inc.
Bloomington

My Phantom Lover

Copyright © 2011 by Carol J. Aken

iUniverse books may be ordered through booksellers or by contacting:

iUniverse
1663 Liberty Drive
Bloomington, IN 47403
www.iuniverse.com
1-800-Authors (1-800-288-4677)

ISBN: 978-1-4620-1919-9 (sc)
ISBN: 978-1-4620-1921-2 (hc)
ISBN: 978-1-4620-1920-5 (e)

Printed in the United States of America

iUniverse rev. date: 06/08/2011

Chapter 1

I was at my parent's home in Green Bay, Wisconsin. I am here for my brother's wedding. I wanted some sunrays before the Wedding I do not get much of a chance with work and all the cases that needed attention.

I feel someone telling to wake up and smell the roses and when I opened my eyes, I could not believe Alex was standing right in front of me and all I could do is stare at him. I was in a daze or am I dreaming I shook my head and ask is that really you Alex?

"He reached out and pulled me into himself and said what happened to my pretty one she went out and got herself all beautiful."

Why would someone not tell me you were going to be coming?

Then he did something I never would expect from Alex, he pulled me right up to himself and kissed me good and proper.

I thought where this come from Alex never let me know how he felt about me! Why now after all these years he never kept in touch with me, or even acted as if he cared about me.

Alex what are you doing after all this time you could not bother to write or even acknowledge me you acted as if I did not exist. I cried my eyes out over you and you just walked away.

Then the dam broke after all these years of hiding my feelings on top of that Richard dying as he did it just overflowed I could not stop crying. Alex was holding me, and he was trying to soothe me, kissing me, and holding me close to him.

"I have been in love with you all our life! Why do you think I hung out with your brother all the time? I did not need to study all that much. I did not need the money I tried to show you how much I loved you, but you just brushed me off as if I was your older brother.

"Alex I can't believe you loved me, I felt like no one cared about me one way or another. I was a middle child who only got in the way. I was always in the way of my siblings and it seemed my parents did not have time for me.

Lizzie shut up and come here and stop, wasting time arguing and kiss me please. I think we wasted enough time what do you think my little beauty?

"Alex I am so sorry you were always there for me and I mistook it for brotherly love.

Then we were wrapped up in each other's arms, I was so happy the tears flowed slowly down my cheeks.

I could not stop kissing Alex and I could not stop the tears. What are we going to do now? My work is in New York, and I do not know where your work is?

"Well sweetheart first of all I want you to do one more important thing.

What is that Alex? First, I want to know if you will marry me.

Alex was down on one knee looking up at me with them big blue eyes, I could swim in and get lost forever. I said yes my darling I will marry you then he slipped the large engagement ring on my finger.

Alex kissed me like there was no tomorrow.

Alex why did you have that ring with you, he said I did not want to take a chance on losing you again, if you said yes I wanted to be ready. I am not letting you out of my sight again. I wondered if I had a chance with you after your brother told me you were a lawyer. Then when he said you would be coming home for the wedding, I ask if you were free? I am going to do everything I can to make her mine. I ask your brother if you were bringing any one home with you. This is when he told me all about Richard, and what had taken place I hope you do not mind.

"I am sorry sweetheart I knew that had to come as a blow to you.

Alex we were friends, not like that, we were just on the same team working to gather. Richard did all the leg - work, I did the paper work. When I found out how jealous his girlfriend was I did not want to work with him at all. I should have been more sympathetic. I could have helped him to get away from someone that needed mental help.

All I know is I let him down, and now he is dead. Shot by a crazy woman who then killed herself. I did not even try to listen to him or offer to help him in anyway. That is pretty sad on my part.

Lizzie how could you know what he was feeling or thinking at the time.

"Maybe he was trying to reach out to her when he knew she needed help.

We cannot go threw life guessing about ourselves all the time. Come on baby take care of your daddy he needs you more than words can say. I love you Lizzie, I need you we have wasted so much time already, Lets make it a double wedding!

"Alex what would Steve and his soon to be wife think about that? I talked it over with them, and they would love that, Steve always knew how I felt about you. "Well you just wait until I see him he could have told me how you felt. I was thinking you would marry someday and I would have to come to your wedding with someone else. I could not bear to see you with someone else, that is why I wanted to be so far from home. I did not want to hear anything about you or your woman friends.

"There was no one that could hold a flicker of a candle to you. I have always loved you and probably always will you are my one and only, my true soul mate.

"Alex, how are we ever going to explain, this to our parents about the wedding.

My head is in a whirl everything was just going so fast. The wedding plans, the dress, the bridal shower. The men wanted to have a bachelor party.

Alex we will not see each other again until after the wedding.

"Who ever made up that cock a mammy rule up? I will not go along with that kind of rule no way I want to be with my girl. Come here Lizzie we are getting out of here!

We left, and got into Alex car, we went to his apartment, and we sat and talked.

Alex said if you only knew how very much I love you.

"I have waited for you seem like all my life, honey please do not be mad at me for wanting to be with you.

"Alex I can not be mad at you I feel the same way.

Alex took me in his arms, and kissed me and ran his tongue around my lips then in my mouth. I felt tingles running up and down my spine. I never knew you could feel this way from a kiss. I was so busy going to college, so I could become a lawyer.

I was working my fanny off, with a job of modeling, so I could support myself.

I did not have a wealthy family; I had to earn my money by modeling. I was so tired from all the running around I had to do. My feet hurt all the time from wearing shoes, those high heels they made you wear to give you height. The only good thing about it was you get to keep all the clothes that I modeled.

I got my mind back to Alex, he was whispering sweet nothings in my ear and suckling on my breast, he was driving me crazy. Alex what are you doing to me?

"I am trying to make love to my fiancée is that alright with you my darling?

Wait Alex I have to tell you something please do not be mad at me.

"What is it sweetheart you can tell me anything?

I have never been with any one before; I have never even been, kissed before you. I had to put my self threw school, so I never had time for nothing else like men I am so sorry honey.

"Sweetheart I am not playing a game I love you, I want you any shape or form, I can have you. Please do not be offended by my need for you it has been so long. Honey I can wait for our wedding if this is what you want? I just love you with all my heart and it is not easy for a man to wait when he is with someone he loves.

Alex we have a lot to discuss before we go any farther. I have my career, and you have yours so what are we going to do about that? I live one place you live somewhere else. I have a job waiting for me, I have worked very hard to get this job, and we really need to talk.

"Lizzie if you are happy living in New York then we will live there. Later if things change, we can talk about that to.

I have only one thing on my mind and that is marring you, and making you all mine. I have waited for you a lifetime and I do not want to mess that up. I will do what ever I have to make you happy my angel.

We waited until the week of our wedding, and I was so happy to be marring my best friend as well as my lover.

The wedding was just beautiful both brides were so happy. I know my parents were happy to see us married and happy.

We had the reception in our father's clubhouse, they had managed to get it decorated from top to bottom it was just perfect. Alex and I put off our honeymoon until we had more time to breathe. I had time to tell my bosses, that I got married. Then I could put in for some vacation time so we could go on our honeymoon.

Alex job took him all around the country he has traveled all over. So I think he would know the best places to go, I kind of had my mind set on Brazil. I heard some very good things about it so we would talk about that when he gets back from his trip.

Chapter 2

❧

I think it took Alex longer on his trip than he thought it would. I was already lonesome for my husband. I never thought I would care for anyone as much as I do for Alex. I hope I can be a good wife to him I do not even know his likes or dislikes. We were just children to gather when we had grown up side by side.

Alex and I grew up next door to each other. Alex was four years older than I was. I felt like he was an older brother to me. Alex always took care of me anything I wanted he would help me to achieve it. If we were at a Halloween party and they were dunking for apples, he would do it for me and hand it to me and he would say for you my pretty. I loved how he took care of me and I knew as long as Alex was around no one dared harm me. Alex was always big for his age and every one knew he could back up anything he said. Alex was and only child and his mother dotted on him. I guess she was never able to have any more children. I never ask Alex why he never had any brothers or sisters I guess it never mattered. I came from a large family of six we had three brothers and 2 sisters I was in the middle. My father and mother worked out side the home. They would leave home with at dawn so we were left on are own. My brother was the oldest so he was in charge he was about the same age as Alex. Therefore, they hung around to gather as they were in the same grade with each other. They both played football on the same team I went to see a lot of him not even trying. I went to all the games as I loved watching them play and I loved the excitement. After the game we all went to the restaurant and had some soda fries, and maybe a hamburger if I had the money. If Alex knew I wanted something and my brother said no, he would go behind my brothers back and get it for me. Alex always called me his pretty I guess it was like a nickname to him, as he never had any siblings. I never thought of Alex as any thing but and older brother who always took care of me. Alex never tried anything with me not even a kiss or a hug and I never thought any more about it.

I had two sisters 2 younger brothers I never worried about anything it just seemed like being alone, unloved, or wanting for anything. I just existed it seemed like the world went around weather I was there or not. I felt like I was so unloved but why I do not know, I have read this is the feelings of an middle child. I felt as if I could do anything and go anywhere no one would notice. My older sisters and brother were the ones responsible for taking care of the younger children. When one of them told me to do something, I usually did what as I told never complained. Alex was over at our house most of the time hanging with my brother Steve. If one of my siblings were, being mean to me Alex would come to my rescue. I loved how he took care of me especially since no one even knew I existed except Alex. I always knew one day Alex and Steve would be going to college and I would be alone with no one to protect me. I really did not want to accept that fact and when that day came, I cried so hard I got the hiccups I ran away so fast I did not want any one to find me. I did not want any one to know how I felt about Alex. I went to my favorite spot, lay down on the grass, and cried my eyes out. I felt like my world took and turned upside down. I was loosing my best friend, as well as the only man I could ever love as well as my brother. I just did not want to face that fact, any member of my family as well as Alex. I felt like a lost soul he was like a brother to me, I did not realize how much I loved him until he moved away. I kept my self busy so I would not think about him so much. When he gets home, we will have to talk about his life and what goes on inside of him that makes him tick.

Alex came home that night and he woke me up very gently with his kisses, and some flowers, and candy, with a bottle of champagne.

"How is my beautiful wife doing?

I missed you baby I do not know if I can handle this being a part time husband.

I do not like leaving my brand new bride, home alone with all these men lurking around her.

We can try for a while and if it proves to be too difficult. I will find a different job, how about that my pretty? Come here I want to make love to my bride.

"He began kissing me all over; I never felt so much love for anyone or anything in my life. I totally gave my self to him heart, and soul.

My man knows how to make love that was for sure.

The next morning I hated going to work and leaving my wonderful husband at home. Nevertheless, duty calls so off I went to the shower. I just gotten my hair wet when my husband came in and said.

"I think I will join you my pretty.

I said wait a minute I cannot see a thing let me rinse my hair, I want to see what my husband looks like all wet. I washed the soap out of my hair and I looked at my very wet husband and said wow my husband looks so fine. I do not know if I can believe my eyes or if this is a mirage. Or if I am dreaming I think I might have to call in for sick day and stay home with my stud muffin how would you like that.

"Oh yeah I like, come here wife I want to make passionate love to you.

We lay around in each other's arm's all day, and night, we ate very little and made love a lot.

I guess we were trying to make up for lost time. I know that might sound silly to some people, but when you are in love you cannot get enough of each other.

I know he will be leaving again, and then I will get back to work. I was not looking forward that being with out my sugar bear. I wanted him all to my self; I was not ready to share him with anyone. I know that sounds selfish, but that is how I feel.

I ask him what he would like for dinner.

"He said how about you on a silver platter my sweet baby; covered with chocolate I could lick my sweet baby all over her body. Well my darling wife how about steak, and lobster with a good bottle of wine?

I think that would keep me in good shape so, I can go on and make my wife happy for the rest of our lives.

After dinner was over, I was laying in my husbands arms daydreaming about when we were children.

Alex and I grew up next door to each other. Alex was four years older than my self was.

I felt like he was an older brother to me, Alex always took care of me anything I wanted he would help me achieve it. If we were at a Halloween party and they were dunking for apples, he would do it for me and, hand it to me and he would say for you my pretty. I loved how he took care of me and, I knew as long as Alex was around no one dared harm me.

Alex was always big for his age and every one knew he could back up anything he said. Alex was an only child, and his mother doted on him.

I guess she was never able to have any more children. I never ask Alex why he never had any brothers or sisters I guess it never mattered.

Chapter 3

When Alex reached down, took my chin, and lifted it up so he could kiss me. I turned over so I could look at him.

He said where you were my darling it seemed like you were far away?

I was my sweet man, I was thinking about when we were children. How you always took care of me, and how I mistook it for brotherly love. I knew after you and Steve left that I had lost someone very special to me, I went to my special place and throw end my self onto the ground and cried my heart out.

Alex I want to get off that subject, I put in for my vacation, just as you ask me to. They gave me the whole month of July, as a wedding present is not that wonderful.

That makes me feel as if I had better put in for mine at for the same time. I might not get the whole month off but I will try.

I feel as thou I am a little kid in a candy store, I am so excited; I can hardly wait for our honeymoon to start. I will have my husband all to my self. When I think about it, it seems like time is dragging by.

I started working harder at my job; my husband has not been home now for two weeks I was getting worried. I picked up the phone called Alex on his cell phone, no one answered. I called his parents they said no they had not heard from there son. What am I to do, I did not know his fellow workers. I decided to get in touch with my brother to see if he had any ideas of where my husband might be.

Steve said he lost touch after Alex got in with the Feds. He went undercover we just did not see each other after that. I went my way and he went his Steve I am so worried about him what am I going to do?

Lizzie quit worrying so much; Alex knows how to take care of himself. You watch he will be coming home then you will know what I am saying is true.

Well a month rolled by and nobody knew any more now then they had when Alex first did not show up.

Mom what am I going to do? I feel like a nervous wreck, I can not concentrate on my job I can't sleep, I am worried sick.

"Well I can only tell you one thing when Alex comes home and finds you looking like a scarecrow what are you going to tell him. I did not have any faith in you after all.

You need to take better care of your self-if not for your self-do it for Alex.

I know he has always loved you so please have some faith in the man.

Mom you are right, I will try to do better at taking care of my self. I went back to work, I throwed my self into my work. I am not going to worry any more; I was working so hard I was not paying attention to the calendar.

Then one morning when I woke up I was so sick, I could not see straight. I went in to shower thinking that would help.

I made up my mind I had the flu, I would try to get threw the day. I thought maybe if I ate something that would help, well that did not work. I was in the bathroom more than at my desk working. I told Ted I was going home, I am to sick to work, I cannot get anything done. I have to get home and lay down for a while then I will work on my case. I fell asleep I was dreaming my husband was making love to me and it felt so damn good. When I woke up of course, I guess I was having one of them wet dreams, I hear people talk about. I never had one before but I have never made love before either so this experience was all new to me. I wonder if it was wise to get married or not. It seems like I am more alone now than ever before, at least I was not hurting like I am now. I still have to face everything alone so what made it any better.

I know Alex loves me but he is not here to hold me or tell me he loves me and damn it all to hell, that means a lot to me. If I am going to be alone all the time I might as well not be married. I am going to tell him so when I see him. This is going to end or our marriage period. I am not going to be married to a ghost. I love you Alex with all my heart, but what is the use if he is not here for me when I am sick. I need him in my life now; I have never depended on anyone all my life.

I think I have a husband to depend on and here I set alone and sick.

Chapter 4

The tears would not stop I fell asleep crying. This is when my phantom lover shows up. I guess he is there for me I am so lonely he shows up to give me courage.

"I like dreaming about him because my husband is never here. I do not understand but I like how he makes love to me. Later that night, I heard something it awakened me to the sound of breaking glass. I got out of bed and was going to see what happened what had made that racket.

Then a big man, with big hairy arms as he cuffed me right along my jaw, attacked me. I could have sworn he broke my jaw, and when I picked myself up off the floor, I seen there was three of them.

Big burly men right out of the movies they were hit men I believe. I could not think of anything they might want from me. I said look I do not have any money laying around here so you are wasting your time on me.

I do not have any jewelry so please tell me what you want and with a little less force please. I am not a strong person.

Look woman we do not want anything from you outside of we want to know where that worthless husband of yours is. If you do not want to loose some teeth, you had better start talking.

I have no idea where he is; I guess the wife is the last person to know where her husband is.

Alex is working undercover, and he cannot tell me where he is. I can see why now to keep ass holes like you away from him that way you cannot beat the answer out of him.

Therefore, I guess you are out of luck fellows you might as well be on your way.

About that time, I felt a boot kick me right in the stomach.

I guess I blacked out about that time.

The next thing I know I woke up in the hospital. I do not know how I got there but I know I was in pain.

I rang for the nurse and tried to tell her I was in pain. My mouth would not open so she asked me if I was in pain. I tried to shake my head yes I could not do that.

She said blink your eyes once for yes and twice for no.

I did what as they ask me to do then I was in dreamland again, and there he was my phantom lover.

He was welcoming me warmly; he was taking such good care of me. I really did not care, if I ever come back from the land of dreams. I would not have my lover, I think this life is much better here at least I am not in pain.

I just surrender my life to my lover because he was so good at what he was doing to me.

I could always count on my dream lover he never left me or caused me any pain or made me cry.

Any time I wanted him all I had to do was go to sleep, and he took care of all the rest. I was so happy here, I never wanted to leave please God let me stay here I am so tired of pain.

I know I was not thinking right, but who cared nobody?

I thought when I got married it was to be a happy occasion but I do not believe there is no happiness here in this world.

I am not budging from my happy place, I know I hear voices but I am not going to respond to them.

I am staying here with my phantom lover; I know he cares about me more than anyone does.

"I heard the doctor saying it is up to her now she has been threw an awful shock, and losing the baby to, must be a horrible thing to a young woman.

I heard Alex, I do not want to lose her Dr. what can I do to help?

"I know this is my fault, and I am not going to harm her again so please tell me what I can do?

Alex just stay with her and talk to her she can hear you so reassure her that all is well. Tell her how much you love her give her a massage; I am sure she is stiff all over.

"Alex; saying how sorry he is about leaving me alone, and with hardly any time spent with me, and not even a honeymoon.

I know exactly how I feel I have gone threw it with out; you do not need to tell me I have been there. I blocked him out he was not promising me nothing I have not heard before I am happy here please leave me alone, Go to your lady love your job, I do not need you or want you good by. I could feel myself sinking deeper and deeper in to oblivion, my lover was taking me with him farther, and deeper than I have ever been but I did not care. I had what no one else has ever given me I am not going back. I know they might miss me but they would soon get over that, and go on with there lives and they can make themselves happy without worrying about me. I do not know how long I was gone but I can assure you my phantom lover knows how to take care of me. I can't fight any more they are winning they are dragging me back. I have fought them as hard as I can what is happening to me. I do not know what they are doing I guess they are winning. My love I will see you in my dreams I will miss you. Elizabeth come on honey please fight we want you back we all love you so much we need you to be here with us. I could hardly open my eyes they kept wanting to stay shut. I said what happened. I cannot open my eyes am I blind? Oh my God this is worse than I thought please let me go I do not want to live please I do not want to be here. I heard

Alex groan please my darling do not say that. I know we have all failed you, I promise we will do a lot better just give us a chance.

I could not bare the thought of him crying for me. I said what the matter Alex

Why are you crying is there something wrong?

Nothing is wrong now my darling, I was so afraid of losing you I prayed for you, and everyone else have been here praying for you.

I took my hand and tried to feel Alex I felt like he was in a tunnel and

I could hardly hear him. Where are you Alex I cannot find you please come closer I want to touch you.

I am right here my angel here take my hand. I know your face is bruised very badly, and you have a concussion, and a lot of broken bones. Please just relax, I will not leave you again I promise. Then I could feel the tears flowing down my face. I am so sorry I just lost our baby Alex.

Elizabeth that was not your fault if any one is to blame it would be me. I left you and I could not get back to you, I am the one that should be sorry.

Will you ever forgive me? I will try so hard to make it up to you. Lizzie as soon as you are feeling better. I will be taking you on our honeymoon we are going to Brazil. Just like you wanted to go we are going to lie around in the sun and make love all day, and night. Right now I just hope you can forgive me and are to feeling better. Alex laid down next to me and was rubbing my arm and talking about what we were going to do when I feel better.

Chapter 5

I started to drift of and my phantom lover was there waiting for me he was beckoning me to come to him. Then I was in my lover's arms and everything else was blocked out. I was at death's door, and all I cared about was being in my lover's arms. When I was here I never worried about anything and I was so happy.

All I know is that they will never leave me alone; they keep pulling me back to the light.

Hold on sweetheart Lizzie come on fight come on fight for us! I need you please come back to me I love you so much.

I hear the agony in his voice I cannot help my self, I do not know why but I decided to come back to Alex he is my husband and I can at least try.

I can always go back to my lover anytime I know he will be waiting for me. I look into Alex's eyes I see all that hurt, I know he is punishing himself and that was not fair.

I knew that when I married him that his job would take him away from me. I guess we never thought about the consequences of his life backfiring in our faces. I said it is all right Alex we will be okay my darling we can start over we can make it so much better.

I love you Lizzie with all my heart. I never want to cause you any harm, or put you in harm's way I am so sorry they did this to you my darling.

Alex did they put them in prison, I want to know if they can come after me again?

They had better hope they stay in prison because if I get my hands on them they might have to lock me up for killing them for hurting you.

When I left the hospital, I was very fearful that some one would wait to hurt me again.

Then Alex took a hold of me and he said come on honey you need not be scared I am here and I am not leaving your side again.

I did not want to be so jumpy but every little thing made me jump and I cannot lie about I was scared. I was having flash backs every night, I would wake up in a cold sweats and shaking like a wet leaf.

Alex tried comforting me but the only place I felt safe was with my phantom lover. When I was there, nobody could hurt me I wanted to go back.

Lizzie I have loved you for so long, and then when I finally get you I leave you alone like an idiot. I do not know where my brain is, I must be nuts, to put you threw all torment I almost lost you. I never will do something so stupid again. I wish I could take away your pain.

When we get to the apartment, Alex opened the door, and I was expecting to see a big mess.

Alex had the apartment redecorated from the windows to the floor. As we walked in the door was our front room. Alex out did himself, I know when there is a crime scene, they have a clean up crew come in, and do there job, but that is all they do.

Alex must have hired a decorator; everything in our front room was new. New curtains, new carpet, he even had bars put on the windows, and on the door, he showed me how the door worked with a remote you can release the locks on the bars, on the windows as well as the door that way in case of an emergency you are not trapped. Although you could not see them, threw the new drapes had them covered, they did let in the sun light. Everything looked fantastic! I hardly recognized our home.

The couch, and the television, was a large 42-inch flat screen. They had it hung on the wall next to the windows, so the light did not shine on the screen. The recliner, looked so good, the color of the new carpet was beige with flex of different colors, in it that brought out the color of the couch, which was a deep brown, the chair matched, and the recliner, was a beautiful color of dark- blue. This brought out the blue in some of the blue in the flex. We now had new end tables, with beautiful lamps. That looked like the old kerosene lamps with beautiful shades over the glass lamp was blue. On the coffee table he had some books laid out with some beautiful pillar candles that was lit. Honey you really out did your self thank you so much. I really do appreciate everything you have done for me.

Alex took me over to a small table that had a drawer in it. When he opened, it there laid a 38 special. Alex I am tired, and I would like to go to rest for a while would that be all right with you?

Sure sweetheart and later I will order some dinner, and I will have it ready when you wake up. Okay honey but remember what I am saying okay if anyone that comes or gives you any trouble you do not ask questions just shoot okay honey?

Chapter 6

Alex fell asleep on the couch watching football. He jumped up so fast when he heard the doorbell, he almost past out from the loss of blood in his head.

I wonder who that could be. He looked out the peephole so he could look out and see who was there. He seen a man out there so he said yes what do you want?

The man said you ordered some food from Fred's diner and I am bringing it to you sir.

Do you want it or not?

Yes, hang on I will get my wallet so I can pay you. Then Alex opens the door and then the man throwed the food at him and grabbed him around the neck.

Alex said what in the name of God do you think you are doing.

He said I am going to kill you. I am making good money for killing you so that is what I am going to do. About that time I heard a shot and I thought I was shot I could not feel any pain.

Then the man fell to the ground, and there stood Lizzie with the gun in her hand shaking all over. I grabbed her and said thank you honey you just saved life.

This man was going to kill me; I cannot believe you shot him.

I called it in and explained what happened they could not believe some one paid to kill you.

You must have pissed some one off if they are paying hit men to kill you. I think we better put you under 24 hour guard.

Good we will need protection until I can get Lizzie on the road to recovery. Mean while I am going to be sticking to her like glue. That is all well, and good but I think Lizzie has been taking care of you.

She certainly did a good job today, yes, she did, and it took a lot out of her. She was shaking so hard, and she could not get warm enough. Therefore, I ran a nice warm bath, and sat with her until she warmed up.

I am putting too much on her she cannot handle all this stress. I think I am going to take a desk job she cannot handle all this war fair.

Please think this over, and take this one day at a time you do not know how Lizzie will take this before you make up your mind.

I will do that I intend not do anything with out her. I will keep Lizzie informed where I stand, and her part in my decision. Well that settles that my boy, I will be on my way then, and you be careful whom you open the door.

I went in and lay down by my lovely wife, and whispered to her. I love you baby do not ever forget that my darling wife, I love you more than life it self. I will do what ever makes you happy, so we can be to gather.

Alex I have always loved you even as a child. I just did not realize how much I loved you until you left me, and never wrote to me.

I am sorry Lizzie I was much older than you were I should have guessed the way you hung around me when you were so little. I just thought you always treated me like your older brother, so I acted the same way. Well I have you now, and I am not letting anything come between us again.

I was so stupid to leave you alone right after we were married and you can bet your sweet butt, I am here to stay.

Alex you cannot give up your career for me and I cannot give up mine neither of us would be happy.

Chapter 7

think I can resolve this matter to where you can have your career and still be with me if you can agree.

Well my beauty what is this plan you have concocted.

I will explain it to you but it has to be our secret no one must find out until we feel safe. Alex and I were feeling much better.

I went into the office and everyone was happy to see me. They were so saddened to hear about the loss of our baby. I was very saddened by that part of my life to, I cannot change any of that right now.

Alex and I would not see each other again, and our lives must go on as usual. I will always love my childhood sweetheart; no one can ever take that away from me. When the papers came out the next day, everyone was asking a million questions.

Why was Alex divorcing you?

I do not know, I guess he just does not love me enough to stay away from his job. I told him it was his job or me. I can only guess what one he chose.

Oh, honey I am so sorry, but I have this friend and he is so good looking. I think you could be happy to gather.

About that time, I started crying, I could not help thinking about Alex.

Honey I am so sorry, I should not try setting you up at this early stage of the game, Can you ever forgive me?

That is all right I am not ready for any kind of date. When I got to my place, there was a message on the telephone saying, I miss you already. I do not know if I can do this, and being away from you is sheer torture.

I took a bath and drank some wine, I was so relaxed, I got out of the tub dripping water everwhere but; I do not care. I just want to get to my bed and fall in it.

I am waiting for my phantom lover to take care of every need. I waited, then I fell asleep, and there he was my lover, and his touch sends shivers down my spine I am so excited. Then his lips were on mine, and I cry out with pure delight. Then he enters me very slowly. A sigh comes from my lips as he sinks deeper in me I think I cannot wait any longer. Then he pulls out clear to the tip of his penis, and then he goes back in slowly, and he repeats this till I am so hot. I don't think I can stand it any longer then he pushes him self way up in my body that is when my head begins spinning. My body goes into a convulsive state, and my vagina wraps around his penis. I felt like I was milking it for all it is worth. My body is shaking, and trembling with such force, I just hoped he could hang on. I felt like a hot poker was inside of me, I wanted all of him I was pushing up, and as far as I could get him in me. I was insatiable the more he gave me I wanted more. Then I wanted hard, and fast he started pumping me as hard, and as fast as he could then we both came as the same time, I held him so tight, and pulled him in to myself. I was ready to go again, I was not satisfied I wanted more. I felt like an untamed creature. I wanted him buried in me so deep, and pushing for all he was worth. I was scratching him, and pulling his hair, and biting him until, I tasted blood in my mouth. I can not believe what this lover of mine does to me, he takes me to places I have never been before, and I love it so much.

As I drift off to sleep, I hear him saying be ready for me my darling. I will be back tomorrow. Then he bends down, and kisses my lips. When I woke up the next day I am thinking why I should have to give him up. He is so good at what he does to me, and I want him again.

That day at work, everyone was saying how tired I looked. I said I do not know what you are talking about; I slept very hard, and had a very restful sleep.

I had a very hard day, and I did not know if I was going to be able to handle it, I was so tired. I think I better get some sleep to night, and forget the lovemaking. I do not know how well my lover will take that bit of news. He wants me every night, I want him to but I cannot get much work done if I keep this up. I had better get my self some good vitamins. I have taken on more of a caseload than usual because I have to stay busy. I will go crazy wondering what Alex is doing out there and if he is okay, I worry about him all the time.

I have this case where a young man accused of raping a young girl. He and his family say he was at home at the time the girl been raped.

I have to prove without a doubt that he is innocent. I hire an investigator to see what he can find out about the girl and the young man.

Mean while I will pursue another case, I am trying to find out what happened to a women that came to me so badly beaten by her husband. She is so afraid of him she does not know what way to go. I make a few calls and try to get her into a shelter but they are all full. I think my only course of action is to take her home with me after all. I just have to get her out of the office with out anyone seeing us. We wait until late and all the office people are gone so no one will know where she is. I hate putting my self in jeopardy with some one's problems.

However, until I can get her in a shelter I do not know any other way out for her. Outside of her going back to her husband and that would not be good next time he might kill her.

We finally get into my car, I have her lay down in the back seat so no one will see her on the off chance some one is snooping around the office. I just want to get inside the garage and into the apartment then I will feel safe. I have the gun and the bars on the windows and the door. Unless someone opens the door, no one can get in so we will be safe.

I just wish Alex were here I would feel much safer.

I make her a bed in the spare bedroom, which was to be the nursery for our baby.

I hope you will be happy here until we can get you somewhere safer I do not want him to find you next time he may end up killing you so please play it safe-and stay put, and quiet.

There is plenty of food, and you have a telephone and a television. I have cable so you should not get bored. I have plenty books you can read if you get tired of watching the boob tube.

I take my bath and read my mail then the phone rang, I about jumped out of my skin. I answered it was the investigator I had hired to follow up on that young girl that was crying rape.

He said he had good information for me could he come over?

I said no, I am too tired tonight; come to my office in the morning I will see you there.

I went to bed I fell right to sleep Then I heard voices. They sounded angry I jumped out of bed my before I could think rationally. I picked up my gun when I entered the front room, I seen Pasty she had let her husband in the door after I told her not to open it for anyone but to come and get me. What is going on here?

Her husband told me to shut your trap bitch. Alternatively, I will give you some of what she is going to get.

I pulled out my gun and I said get your ass out of my apartment. Pasty if you wish to go with him go but never come to me for help again do you hear me young woman.

About that time, he launched out at me before I knew what was happening. I shot him he fell at my feet. I screamed for Pasty to call for an ambulance and all she could do was scream hysterically.

You killed my husband now what am I to do I cannot live without him.

When the police got here, I filled them in on what was going on.

She said you killed him in cold blood that he never stood a chance with you.

Well all I know is that he came at me and calling all kinds of names. And said he was going to give me some of what he was going to give his wife when he got her alone.

I do not know what her problem is I have done everything in my power to protect her from him she came to me for help.

I did not go looking for her that is for sure.

Well we will investigate and see what we can come up with but do not leave the city limits.

Well I do not think you have to worry about that officer, my practice is here.

I have several cases pending so you know where you can find me.

I went to sleep that night I tossed and turned all night long.

I never even had any use or time for my lover. I could not get enough sleep so he could come to me.

I kept seeing the scene happening repeatedly I was wondering what I could have done differently but no matter how I looked at it there was nothing more I could have done.

I finally fell asleep at the exact time that I needed to get up and go to work.

I had an appointment so I had to be there.

I drank a pot of coffee but it did not help. I felt all out of sorts and I would be so happy when this day would end. I was to have a ten o'clock meeting and I hope he had some good news for me I sure needed something good to happen for a change I was so sick of my life, was in at this time.

The next day they informed me; I was to report to the closest police station. When I got to the police station, I reported to the desk clerk that I was to report to the captain.

He told me to have a seat he would be right with me. While I am waiting, I got a hold of the investigator that I had hired to tell him I would not be able to see him at our appointed time. I would call him as soon as I was free. Finally, the captain came out and called me into his office. He motioned me to have a chair. I am curious what is this concerning; He said that a Mrs. Pasty Ann Woodrow has brought charges against you.

I just need to ask you in your own word what happen on the night that her husband shot.

I told him what had happened;

He said you think that woman would be happy you did her a favor.

I looked up her record on her and her husband it seems they have a record of abuse on both sides. I am going to tell her, she had better settle down. I might have to arrest her on charges of wasting my time and yours.

Chapter 8

I was so happy this was over and I can get back to work. I have wasted too much time already. I called my Investigator, and ask him if we could do lunch. He told me he would be there. I seated my self next to the window. I could see him as he walked by I was watching the people walking by. I would try guessing what kind of life style they might have. I even tried to guess what there occupation would be if they were a Dr. or nurse, housewife, preacher, race car driver it was kind of fun.

I new I probably was not right but it helped pass the time away. I spot Don coming up the sidewalk he was a very handsome man. I think to my self, I bet he never has any problems getting information he probably has women falling at his feet.

I was anxious to hear what kind of information he might have for me. I knew he seen me so I motioned him over to my table. I ordered a bottle of wine the waiter took our orders as we waited for our food he began to fill me in on what he had learned about our sweet little innocent girl it seemed was not so innocent after all.

She had in another State tried to file rape charges against another young man. She had tried to extort money for her injuries. They refused to pay she had threatened to take him to court they had told her to go ahead and nothing ever came of it.

Well it seems as if the worm has turned and finally something has started going my way. We sat eating our lunch I told him how happy I was that he could turn up some good news for our side. I looked over at him, and he seemed to be in deep thought, I ask him if there was anything, I could do for him in any way?

He looked up at me with very sad eyes, and said that he had just lost his young wife to cancer.

He has gotten over the ordeal he told me how she had suffered how he sat by her bed day and night.

I said I am so sorry, I had no idea or I would not have bothered you.

He said oh no I need the work to keep my mind off it or I might go crazy. Moreover, I have an outstanding hospital bill; I need to pay off so I am so pleased that you called on me.

Don I would like you to consider working for me full time? What would the work consist of?

I explained it all in full detail, what the pay would be.

He said he would be happy to work for me, and he hoped that I could keep him busy.

I said that would not be a problem you will be begging me to stop working him so hard.

I filled him in on another job that was demanding my attention. I ask him if he would take care of for me. I then ask him how much I owed him, and I was writing out the check. I seen some one coming up from my side I looked up to see Pasty standing there staring daggers at me.

I ask her what her problem was.

She said if you think for one minute that I am going to forget what happened you are crazy.

I said for your own sake you had best be on your way before I bring charges against you.

I can and I will put your ass in jail if it comes down to that. So be on your way before I change my mind and have you arrested right this minute for stocking me.

Don asks me what in the hell was she trying to prove by harassing you?

I filled him in and when I was finished, he said my God what is her problem?

You probably saved her life and all she can do is threaten you.

Well what can I say; I tried to help her I guess some people you just cannot help.

Well Don I think I am going to like working with you. I am happy with what you have done for me in this case. I want to thank you so much, Don handed me the paper work.

I would be seeing the young man later on that same day him.

His parents I know they will be happy I have information to back her down. I know she will more than be happy to drop this case. My next big case was a murder case where a woman stabbed her husband to death. Then tried to hide his body she had put his body in his car, and drove it off a ravine into the water; she had hoped no one would discover the body or the car.

I needed to talk with her to get her story. I packed my brief case, and was on my way out when the phone rang.

I said yes, how might I help you then there was silence I said who is this? If you do not answer, I am hanging up.

Then I heard Alex, say how are you honey? I am sorry to bother you but I cannot stand it any longer. I need you baby please can I see you tonight?

Alex, I would love to see you to, you have a key just let your self in. Alex you do not have to call me first after all I am your wife I love you.

Alex if you get there before me help yourself until I get there.

I have to go and get a deposition from a Clint. Then I will be home my darling as soon as possible I miss you so much. Then I was on my way to the jail where my Clint, is. I could not wait to get home, as I knew my husband would be waiting for me. I also had to get this information taken care of or I could lose the case that would not be good for my Clint or me.

I had to keep my mind on what I am doing then when I am done, I can concentrate on my man.

It seems that all we do is live are lives apart I always thought that when I got married we would live a quiet life, and have a couple of children and all would be normal.

Chapter 9

I should have known better, my life has not been normal since the day I was born. What more could I expect I guess I will do as I have always done just go on with my life and let everything fall into place.

I finally got to the prison they called my Clint in and I took her deposition. I told her that if I find out that she has lied to me in any way. I would drop her like a hot potato. My next step was to give this out to my investigator and hope we could get this case in to court.

I finally got home, I could hardly wait to get to my husband, I any more than got to my door it flew open he grabbed me, and pulled me into his big strong arms, and was kissing me all over.

We were tarring at each other's clothes in a heated frenzy, all the while his lips never left mine.

I could hardly breathe when we finally had our clothes off he picked me up, and put me on the bed, and slowly made love to me.

I was thinking to my self, I thought my phantom lover could make love wow. Boy was I wrong my husband had it over on him he was no match for my husband. How could I ever think someone else was any better than my husband was?

I love you Alex, I hate us being apart how long can we go on like this my darling?

Liz remember this was your idea not mine. I know my darling.

I just want you to be happy if you are not doing as you wish then you would not be happy would you?

I have a big court case, and you would not be happy with me being gone all the time would you? I love you, and you are doing what makes you happy as well as my self.

I wish we could be to gather. I just feel so cheated, as if life has just over looked us, when it comes to happiness.

Well honey I guess we go on like always and hope for the best right?

Unless something else comes up and I will pray for us that, we can always be to gather and start a family if we do not wait to long.

How long do we have before you have to go?

Well would you believe we have a whole week so let us not waste time and let us make love, and enjoy each other?

I will help you any way I can, I will cook, and clean do the laundry, the dishes. I just want to make your life as easy as possible how that sounds to you. I wish I could do so much more for you and if it was possible,

I would go out and slay the entire dragon's for you that had giving you a bad time how does that sound?

Well mister eager beaver take a good look at this next case file. While I take a bath then we can discuss it if you would not mind.

I sure could use some help on this one, I cannot tell if she is lying to me or not, and all the evidence is pointing right at her. I sure would appreciate all the help I can get so what do you think can I count on you?

I would love to look this over then when you get back, we can discuss it. Liz is you sure that you do not want me to take a bath with you? I could wash your back, and you could wash mine then we can go on from there.

Well mister smarty-pants, I would just love that but I do not think we would get anything done if we do that.

Alex please let me have my way this once.

I will gladly do things your way baby. I took my bath, and when I came out Alex had set up a nice bottle of wine he lighted up some candles.

I said well Mrs. Miller I already could tell you this much I do not think she is guilty because someone has taken a lot of time and energy to set her up. Now all you have to see is who can gain the most from all this.

The next day I got a hold of my investigator, and told him to look into who would gain the most from the death of the woman's husband.

When I reached my office and got to my desk the phone is ringing. When I answered, I heard my husbands voice I said hello my sweetheart what is up with you baby.

I was just wondering what you would like for dinner my love?

I said honey why not surprise me I love surprises. Well then do you have any idea of what time you might be home, or are you going to surprise me on that?

I do not know what time I will be done, but I will let you know as soon as I know okay.

I am sorry that I cannot say any more than that as of this time. I do not even know myself it just means, I will get home as soon as possible. When I was done with my hectic day, I was so tired.

Then that delicious aroma hit my nostrils as it pulls me into the kitchen. I said wow what is that delicious aroma.

Alex was smiling ever so shyly he said it is your favorite my darling you remember. I said I sure do not remember that beautiful aroma so what is it?

Well my darling since you do not care to venture a guess, I will have to show you. Come over here and have a seat, I will serve you a fine glass of wine, and some nice candle light then I will bring you your first course.

That is when he served some creamy cheesy broccoli soup. Then Alex said I have a small salad served with a light vinaigrette and oil. When you have finished that I will serve the main course then that is when he brought out the biggest lobster tail I have ever seen and a candle with hot steamy butter.

I said I must have died and went to heaven, this is delicious oh my God, thank you honey you just made my day.

When I first came home, I was so tired I thought I could just bathe and go to bed.

Well my pretty I have arranged a nice, relaxing bath, and some soothing music, a nice glass of champagne, how does that sound?

I have laid out a nice negligee then when you are finished with your bath we will dance until we fall into the bed together.

Alex how can I ever thank you my darling, you just made my day, I wish we could live like this everyday, I miss you so much. I know honey but with your hours and mine and the danger.

Elizabeth, I want you to be safe, and out of harms way.

I miss-you to, it just the same it seems as thou we do not even have a marriage.

I cannot talk about you to my co-workers.

I have to put on a show as if you do not exist, and do you know how hard that is?

Everyone is trying to set me up with there brother, or friend, of the family.

Honey this is not much fun for me either, I miss you so much, I have to control my self to keep from wanting to come in here, and tear your clothes off.

Well what is stopping you? Alex you can come, and go as you please you have a key.

You know very well what is stopping me I do not want someone following me in here and hurting you like before.

Alex how could anyone get in this is like a Fort Knox wit bars on the windows and doors. Honey please come home I need you to be my husband. Elizabeth I will as soon as I know where I am at right now I cannot risk it.

We lay in each other's arms all night, I knew he would not be here long, and then I would be alone with my phantom lover. I guess if I cannot have the real thing, I would have him.

I needed to get up early the next morning and get busy on my cases. At least I can keep busy helping other's that need my help. Weather it true or false that was for the courts to figure out. My job is to present there case to the best of my ability so that is what I must do.

I work very hard for my client and I have always been interested in making sure the poor get justice as well, making sure the poor get justice as well as the rich, I will donate as much of my time to those that cannot afford a lawyer as well as those who can.

When I woke up Alex was gone he left me a note on the cupboard with a pot of coffee, he left a large sum of money.

He said please put this money in the bank for our future, I love you with all my heart, and soul, we will be to gather soon, please be patient, and take care of your self for me. I will be in touch, and I will always be watching out for you. I love you with all my heart and I always have since we were children.

Well I decided to work hard and do my best for my clients, I called my private eye Don, to see what he had for me he said meet me for dinner, and we can discuss this case.

We met at a small but discreet restaurant, so we could get down to business.

When I finally reached the restaurant, Don was already seated he had picked a large table in the back of the room so we can talk.

He asks me if I wanted anything to drink, I said yes I want a vodka Gimlet. After the server took our order, he began trying to fill me in on what he had learned; well here is where we are.

I am so anxious to hear what you have found out.

I did some digging in on who has the most to gain and it seem he had a girl friend, and she has taken out a million dollar insurance claim.

I checked even further and it seems she has another boyfriend, and she has a million dollar claim on him as well.

I reached him and began asking him some questions; it seems he does not know anything about her having an insurance claim on him.

W e will be going to sup-peony him into court as well as the other woman. I do not know how I can thank you for all your hard work,

Hey, you pay me good money to do a job that I love doing.

After we had our dinner he said how about an after dinner drink?

I said I would love one and then I will have to be gone. I just want to fall into a bed and get a good nights sleep. I will be talking to you tomorrow and thank you for working so hard for me.

When I reached my door, I seen someone standing there watching me, I reached for my cell phone and called 911 then I waited for the police to come. When they got there, they found the man and ask him what he thought he was doing just standing around on someone's property?

They arrested him and called to let me know he would not be a bother any more tonight.

What had just happened frightened me, and I needed someone to talk with so I called Don and ask him if he would mind if we just talked for a while.

He said sure what is the matter and how can I help? I said if you would please check that man out and see where he hails from.

He scared the shit out of me, I feel like I am in danger, please just checks him out for me.

All right Elizabeth, I will go right down and see what I can get, and check, him out I will get back with you tomorrow, and let you know what I find out.

I decided to try to get a bath and then to get a good nights sleep, and put all my thoughts on him. That is my phantom lover is always around to come to my rescue. When I was ready to fall asleep, there he was ready willing to take my troubles away. He made love to me as if I could never believe possible even in my dreams.

I had a very good nights sleep, and I was ready to start my day. I had a big day in court today, and I have to give it my best to get an innocent girl out of prison.

Don showed up and I was so happy to see him I knew we had this case sewed up. With all the evidence, he had, and the witnesses he had dug up this was going to be a slam-dunk. We were waiting for the jurors to get back in.

I ask Don, to let me know what he had found out about the person that was outside of my place.

I found out he is not a very nice person. He has a record as long as my arm. If I was you I would get a protection order then if he shows up they will be able to him arrested.

Then my beeper went off, we have to go back in the jury is back.

When I got back, the courtroom was called to order by the bailiff, and the Judge asked the jury if they had come to an agreement?

They responded with yes we have then they handed it to the Bailiff he in turn handed it to the Judge. The Judge handed it back to the Bailiff he in turn handed it to the foreman of the jury. The Judge said how do you find the Defendant we find her innocent of all charges against her.

She grabbed me and hugged me so hard I could not breathe.

I said if it were not for Don here, I could not have won this case.

He is the one that all the dirt on the people that are actually guilty.

The prosecuting Attorney will take over and bring charges against both of them and I am out of here.

Wait up Elizabeth I need to talk to you I am so worried about something. They let that fellow out of jail; I wish you would come home with me until I can find out more about him.

Don if you would just see me home, I will be safe at my home it is fool proof to any burglars.

The last time I was attacked my husband made it safe for me while I was in the hospital.

That is when I lost my baby, and almost lost my life. I was in a coma for almost a year. I did not much care to come back to this messed up world. I was a big mess after I found out I lost our baby! Well Don came home with me and walked me to my door, I ask him if he wanted to come in and have a drink?

H e said no it is getting late, and I have a big day tomorrow but I will take a rain check.

After I got my bath taken, and settled in for a good nights sleep then the phone rang.

I reached for the phone and about that time, a hand grabbed my hand and about scared the living daylights out of me.

I screamed and then his mouth closed over mine silencing me to a groan then he pulled me up into his arms and still kissing me greedily. I tried to fight him off but, I did not stand a chance of getting free he was too big and had hard muscles.

Then I realized that it was Alex, I thought well you ass hole. I could kill you for scaring me like that Alex said he did not have a choice some one is watching you very closely and I want to find out who he is, and what does he want from you?

I am so sorry honey but I did not want to scare him off.

I have a bunch of the guy's that I work with and they are going to grab this little fellow, and find out what is going on with his little world.

I lay in my husbands arms wondering how he knew someone had been bothering me.

I ask, Alex how did you know about the person I just had him picked up yesterday.

They told my associate that he free today.

I thought he had learned his lesson and moved.

Well I hate to tell you this sweetheart, but he is lurking right outside your window. I spotted him when I when I was trying to sneak into our house without him seeing me.

Then if he tries anything, I can handle him. I have the men watching him right now so let us enjoy this night to gather.

The next morning my husband was gone just like a thief in the night.

Chapter 10

I could not believe he showed up like that, I went into the kitchen to have some coffee, and see what was on the television.

Then I seen the note we got that Grimy little son of a bitch you will not have to worry about him again.

I love you sweetheart, and I will always take care of my little pretty one. I must say I did feel a lot better knowing I did not have to worry about him again thanks to my husband.

I was about to go out my door when my phone rang, I answered it and the phone went silent. No one was there now; I was beginning to wonder what was going on now.

I was out the door and then I seen Don he was about to ring the doorbell.

I said what is up Don. H e said I really do not know, I was about to ask you the same thing.

Do you remember that fellow that was bothering you? Well I guess no one can seem to find him so do you have any knowledge of what is going on.

I have not heard any thing Don. I was about to start my day when, I seen you out here.

Well do you have anything for me; I really want to keep busy.

I just do not like setting around to long I begin to think too much.

Don gives me a chance to get to the office and check my calendar, and see what I have scheduled for today.

I will call you as soon as I know what is going on and then we both can get busy.

I reached my desk and the phone was already ringing.

I answered with you have reached the desk of Elizabeth Miller how may I help you?

That is when I heard the faint moans of what sounded like a man.

Please how can I help you, I cannot help but wonder if it is Alex trying to get a hold of me.

What if that same man that was following me caught up to him, no that can't be Alex said his men were taking care of that, and he stayed with me.

What if it is some kind of Gang and they have Alex. They are trying to get information from him?

However, what would Alex have that they want?

God I do not even know what kind of work my husband actually does for his company.

We forget to talk about where he works and what kind of work he does.

I am so concerned about Alex that I am having a hard time concentrating on my work.

I am wondering why does not get a hold of me and let me know what is going on with him. If I was not so worried, I could really be mad at him for making me worry like this.

I could shoot him my self, and I still might if he does not get a hold of me damn soon.

I need to get to work and stop thinking about my husband. I need to concentrate on my job that way I will not be hurting some one else with my mistakes.

I cannot really talk about any of my problems concerning my husband because they all think we are divorced.

I am all alone on this one, and I do not like it one little bit what am I going to do about this, I ask myself.

I finally get to my desk and I look to see what kind of case I need to get right on.

I will need to keep busy so I can quit thinking about Alex, Oh my god what if I was in trouble what would Alex be doing?

I bet he would not just sit and worry about things would he.

I have to find out what is going on; I will not leave one stone unturned. I need to find out what has happened to him.

I do not care who knows, I love my husband I call Don and tell him what is going on and I need his help.

Don said, I would do what ever I can, just tell me where you want me.

I am going to check all the hospital's would you check the police and call me.

I did not know anyone that Alex worked with but I knew his phone number so I called his phone. When no one answered, I was so mad. I just stood up and screamed bloody murder.

I knew this did not help but I did not know what else to do,

I did not know what way to go, I did not know anything about my husband those were the facts. I have never been a Detective but there is a first time for everything.

I need to put in for some time off so I can spend more time looking for my husband.

I know if something were wrong with me, Alex would do everything in his power to get to me.

Don I need your help as soon as possible, I went to my partners and told them everything right from the start.

I said I am so sorry for not telling you all the truth but, I was in so much danger; Alex thought it best if we told everyone we had gotten a divorce. That way that ever was after Alex would leave me out of the equation.

After I explained everything, everyone was saddened that I could not trust or her but they understood.

They all agreed if I needed anything at all to reach them anytime day or night.

I thanked them all I was sobbing hysterically by the time I left.

Don met me coming down the stairs and wanted to know what is going on?

Come with me I need you to help me find my husband!

I took time off from my work so I can devote all my time to finding Alex he is in serious trouble. I received a phone call this morning and I believe it was Alex and he could not talk he sounded like he was in so much pain.

Well if you are serious about this, I will help you as much as possible, but I have to tell you this could be very dangerous for the both of us do you understand this Elizabeth?

I do, I know, Alex would do the same thing for me and he has.

Don I need to know where do we begin?

I am going to try to put a tap on your phone, and see if I can get them to let me know where that last call came from.

Mean while you go home, and stay there. I come and get you as soon as I get some things worked out at the police station.

I am going to set up some planes we can go by.

So find some old clothes to wear, as we might have to do some hiking and wear comfortable shoes or boots.

One thing we do not need to worry about is how we look.

I wish you could dress more like a man then some beautiful debutante okay.

This is just a suggestion it is not set in gold or anything okay.

Lizzie if it is all right for me to call you by that name it will help.

I will be back in a couple of hours and if you need anything please call me other wise I will be back as soon as possible.

I gather up all my old ragged jeans and old sweatshirts, and old underwear, and fill up a backpack. I go to the closet to find some old boots and stockings.

Then I spot some of Alex old hat, and I decided to wear them and I put my hair in a ponytail, and looked in the mirror to see if I could pass my self off as a man.

I went to the bathroom to take off all of my makeup and lost my earrings.

I looked for the gun that Alex had left me for my protection. I found one of his shoulder holster's, I fit it to my self and put the gun in it and then I put on one of my old jackets that I had worn to do gardening in actually it was one of my brothers.

I said to my self, I think I can do this; I laid down to rest until Don got back.

I fell asleep that is when my dream man came to me and oh, my God he did look mighty fine all bronzed from his head to his naked toes.

I put my arms out for him to come to me and he smiled and winked.

Then he pulled me into his muscle bond arms.

I feel like I can not breath he is so handsome God, I knew he was going to take me right then and there and I wanted every minute of it to last forever. I do not know how long I slept so soundly I did not here the phone ringing then all of a sudden, I snapped right straight up in a daze from waking up so fast like that my mind could not focus on what was going on. Then I heard the phone ringing I said hello and then I heard Alex screaming at the top of his lungs.

Alex please tell me where you are I will come to you, and then I heard more moaning and groaning.

I start to cry and that is when I heard a voice telling me If I ever wanted to see my husband again, I had better not call the police or the feds, I did not know what he was talking about. I said as far as I know there is no police officers involved or feds but. I will try to find out what is going on please do not hurt Alex I will do anything please.

By the time Don got there, I was a mess from crying; he looked at me and asked me what the matter was?

I told him what had taken place and he said this is a lot deeper than I had first thought.

I don't know Lizzie: I think you should back off and do as they said, I am afraid for you, I can handle myself: and I am paying you to help me so let's get started, you can fill me in on what you have found out.

Alex always made sure I was fully prepared or the worse. I learned karate, I also have my own gun I do know how to use it.

I went to the range where the police officers go, and they were very helpful.

I have already shot two men one more does not matter as long as I can get my Alex back safe and sound. Now are you with me or against me I have to know if I can count on you?

All right, I am hear for you, and I will do everything I can to help you get your husband back.

Now where do we start? I have some addresses we can check out.

I am going to knock on the door and ask if so and so live there this way maybe, I can get entrance into the house and see what is going on in there. Otherwise, we are starting from scratch, well that is better than nothing is right.

We took Don's car that way no one would think anything about it, as we drove up to that house. I got a cold chill right up my spine I said please be careful.

Don does not take any unnecessary chances I do not know that.

Please do not worry about me; I will not do anything to put our lives in danger okay?

Don went up to the door and knocked and there was no response. So he knocked a few more times then he went around back to look into the window. I was waiting for him to come back that is when I seen the car pulls into the driveway.

I crouched way down in my seat and dialed Don's cell no. but I got no response. I decided to go and look for him as I went around the corner, I seen one of the men knock Don on the head.

One man said to the other one whom do you think he is? Probably one of them undercover cops I suppose, I thought what can I do to save Don then I said honey where are you? Is anyone home? Honey come on lets get out of here we can come back later to see if Julie still lives here. I seen the men drop Don and go back into the house as I came around the corner. I screamed Don are you all right come on let us get out of here we can come back tomorrow.

Don said what happened. I said, I do not know, come on maybe they will be here tomorrow, we can come back if you are feeling up to it.

I told Don what had happened, and he could not believe they let him go without an argument.

I told him what I had done, and he said thanks,

I guess I owe you my life now what are we going to do?

I think we should stay here and see if they go anywhere. If they do, I can tail them and you can get another look in the house.

I just have a bad feeling about that house.

I think there is something going on that they do not want anyone to know what it is.

Don if you are up to this you will have to be very careful, and for goodness sake turn your cell on vibrates in case I have to get a hold of you please.

We sat in the car until morning my body had a cramp in it I really needed to stretch. I knew that was not going to happen so I tried to stretch out my legs without waking Don up.

I lay still so Don could rest and he had not stirred at all.

I rose up for enough to see if the car was still there and it had not moved at all.

I said Don is you awake yet. I got no answer I raised up to look into the back seat and it was empty. I think oh my god where did that man go off. I was wondering if I should call him or just wait.

I am sure he did not just go off and leave me here all alone. Then I seen a dark shadow moving along side of the house. I am shaking from the top of my head to my very toenails. I feel like a wet dog shaking for the fear of my life, after someone scolds them for doing something wrong.

I am laying low in my seat so as not to be seen when I heard Don say its me open the door, I looked up and seen that it was Don and then I was so relieved.

I could have kissed him if I was not so dam mad. What in the hell are you doing are you trying to get us killed or what are you thinking about going off like that on your own?

Listen to me, I went around back to see if I could look in the window, and see what is going on but it was dark and I could not hear a thing.

I guess we will have to wait and see what they will do tomorrow. Should I this morning I laid back down to see if I could sleep for a while longer then. I heard a noise it seemed they were going to be on the move really early. I said Don Do you see what I said yes I am stay put until they get themselves situated.

Then we can see what is going on remember if they leave you stay on there tail. Let me know where they are going and I will check out the house as he slipped out of the car.

I am saying a silent prayer that God will be with me and guide me to where my husband is and that I can be of some help to him and not a hindrance.

Then I hear the motor start up so I wait a while then I drive away very slowly with my lights off so they will not notice me following them. After we get on the highway, I turn off into a driveway so I can get my lights on and they will not see me.

Then I back out very slowly and begin following them at a safe distance. I believe were heading into the countryside. I need to keep the taillights in view so I will not loose them. There is no traffic tonight so I pray nothing happens please God help me to stay strong my hands are shaking so hard I can hardly keep them on the steering wheel.

I turn back off my lights and follow them about five miles down a dirt road. Then I lost track of where they might have gone so I sit and wait to see if I can hear anything. Then I heard the voices loud and clear I guess they felt safe enough to talk, loud seeing as to how there were no neighbors around to hear them.

I slowly get out of the car and shut the door softly; I did not want to make a sound.

I tried to take my time and get as close as possible without them hearing or seeing me. I walked very softly so as not to snap a tree branch or to fall over something. I made my way to one of the windows so I might peek in but the room was dark and I could not hear a sound so I waited and hugged the wall until I could hear something.

I think they are leaving and I cannot take my car without them seeing me oh no what have I done now?

Then I thought maybe I can find something out from inside the building maybe they left a clue of some kind.

I waited for about a half an hour to make sure no one was still there.

Then I made my way around to the front of the building, and I tried the door and it opened with a squeaking noise.

I could just make out a table and chairs and then I saw Alex laying on the floor bleeding about his head, I thought he was dead for sure. I got down on my hands, and knees, and whispered Alex my darling please wake up and the tears were falling.

I said oh God please let him be all right I ran and got a rag, and some water, and washed his face and I want to see if he is breathing but I could not tell. I just start crying please God let him be all right. I do not know how long I sat there holding Alex I heard my phone ringing and when I answered it was Don I said oh Don I forgot all about you I found Alex and he is hurt bad please come and help me get him some help. I managed to tell him where I was.

Then about that time in walked the burly man that looked like he never took a bath or shaved. I thought oh my God now we both are going to die for sure. What in hell are you doing here? Get up and take a seat while I get a hold of my boss and tell him what I found creeping around this house. I said please just let me take my husband and leave here. I will not say a word about anything please he needs a Doctor or he will die then you will be charged with murder and I know you do not want that do you? Well about that time, the lights went out. I could not remember what had taken place and what I was doing here.

I was wondering sir what is going on I just woke up and I do not know what is going on please tell me how did I get here and who are you and what happened to that man on the floor? I need to get home my parents will be wondering where I am so please call me a taxi so I can get home please.

Chapter 11

All of the sudden the door flew open and these big burly men in suits came in. What are you doing here; please just let us go we will not say anything. About that time I was hit on the head and the lights went out. The next thing I know there are police officers and some other fellows standing over me. That man on the floor he looked like he needed help. They were asking me so many questions that I could not answer I said why are you asking me all these questions when you should be getting this man some help.

I said I do not know what you are talking about I do not even know these men nor should I say police officers.

Elizabeth what is wrong with you? Have you lost your mind you called me and told me where you were? I do not even know who you are sir? There is a very sick man over there on the floor that needs help. Why are you even talking to me when he may die waiting on you to get him some help?

Elizabeth you are having some problems to so you need to go to the hospital along with Alex. You have blood on the side of your head I do not have blood on my head. I need to have a look I never felt any pain if I was hit you think I would have some kind of recognition of that fact right? Please let look into a mirror I cannot believe somebody would hit me. What did I do to deserve that I never hurt any one in my life on this earth.

I cannot believe somebody would deliberately hit me on the head; I just do not know what I am doing here how did I get here any way? I have been trying to tell you we were looking for your husband and you were following the men that had him. Then I do not know what you did but you did find your husband and that is he lying on the floor. There is an ambulance on its way and I want you to go with your husband to be looked at okay?

I just want to go home to my parents; I bet they are worried about me. I do not know how long I have been gone but my parents will be worried.

When we got to the hospital they put Alex right in the intensive care unit, unit and they checked out Elizabeth then put her to bed and they told her they would get a hold of her parents, and let them know what is going on.

The federal boys had the one man they could work on him to try to figure out what was going on and why he beat up Alex and hit Elizabeth on the head.

Until such a time we are all in the dark about what went on? I will keep looking and I will stay real close to Alex and Elizabeth I just want to make sure no one gets close enough to harm either one. I also had them put on a 24-hour guard, to make sure no one got close enough to hurt them in there weakened condition.

About a month later, they had released Elizabeth so she could go home to her parent's home.

Elizabeth had still not gained her memory and she does not remember anyone after a while of being in the country she had regained her physical being, and she looked wonderful.

She took long walks along the hillside and she would take a blanket with her so she could stretch out in the sunshine.

Some days she would just lay there as if she was in a trance daydreaming about what only she knew the answer to that question.

I was wondering if she was ever going to snap out of her own little world or maybe she did not wish to come back to such a violent world that she had suffered so much loss in.

Alex was coming along slowly I cannot believe any man could take such a beating and still have any sign of a brain left in his head.

I guess the good Lord was protecting the both of them from so much violence and hurt by putting her in a state of amnesia so she would not remember the entire heartache she had put up with all her life.

Alex had lost consciousness so he could not know what was going on with his body all the punishment that they put on that poor man.

Chapter 12

One year later Alex had made so much improvement and he was insisting on getting out of the hospital. I knew I had to tell him that when he would get home he would not have a wife waiting there patiently for him.

I hate my job as of now, I hate being the barer of bad news but I guess someone has to do it.

After I told Alex the bad news he just shook his head and said all I have ever done is bring that poor woman trouble.

Well no more, I am leaving her to live her life without me causing her more pain.

I will just do what I am good at and find the people that have done this to the one woman that I have loved with all my heart.

I do not know how you can walk away and leave her after she gave up everything to find you even her memory.

I just do not want her to be hurt because of me now that would be unfair.

I want her to go back to her old life and to forget about me that is the end of this subject.

I was very saddened by what Alex was proposing, I could not see how he could just up and walk away.

I know with all my heart if she was mine I would not let her out of my sight for fear someone would come and take her away from me and I could not stand for that.

Good God look at me thinking, I would even have a chance with someone like her.

When I got back to see how Elizabeth was doing her parents met me at the door with horrified looks on there face's.

Don, Elizabeth is gone we have looked all over for her. We are thinking some thing awful has happened to her what shall we do?

I asked them if they had gotten a hold of the police.

They both said yes but they will not do anything until 24 hours are up. They cannot do a thing.

Don do you think those men have gotten a hold of her. I am afraid they might kill her thinking she might know where Alex is.

Please take it easy, I have some good friends on the police force. They owe me some favors.

I will talk to them and I will get back to you when I know something, mean while quit worrying and start praying.

I neither do nor know what I am talking about I have not one clue to where Elizabeth might be. For all I know maybe she just wondered off and got her self-lost this sort of thing happens all the time.

Well I called in all of my favors with what good it did me. I know even less now than I did before I had talked to my friends.

They promised if they heard or had any news of any sort. They would get back to me. I went to where Elizabeth always went and laid on the ground, thinking maybe I could get some kind of mind set on to where Elizabeth had went or what she might have been thinking.

I just laid in the sun and just gave in to self hypnotic state of mind. I fully surrendered my self to see if I could get some kind of reading on what this beautiful lady might have been doing or thinking. I felt so warm and then my beautiful woman came to me dancing across my body like a weightless image dancing and singing. Oh, my darling where have you been everyone is so worried about you. You need not worry I am safe but I am so sorry I made you worry. Then she pressed her lips to mine and I thought I was going to lose it right then. Elizabeth I never thought you could care about me?

Well Don that goes to show you not to think so much, it is not good for you and it is all wrong come my darling make love to me. I need you so much, I feel so safe when I am in your arms, and you are my hero.

I gave her everything I had and when we were finished, we both were drained and soaking wet with sweat.

I whispered I love you, I just do not know what I would do if I lost you now my darling.

You are so silly my big worrywart, I am yours any time you want me, I am right here next to your heart and do not forget that. Then she kissed me long and hard now anytime you want me I will be right here waiting for you my very own sweetheart.

I laid there for it seemed like and eternity; I would love having Elizabeth as my very own, but I did no the difference between real, and daydreaming; but if that is all I can have then I will take what I can get and be thankful for it.

I do not any more now than when this all came about. Then it happened; I seen a mirage of Elizabeth and she was motioning me to her self, I seamed to think she wanted to tell me something: then I hear in a small little voice quit worrying about me, I am just fine please: I just do not need this so please quit: before someone gets hurt.

I am here for you my darling: for the rest of our lives, I will never give up on you.

Elizabeth awakes and finds her self-bound: from her head to her feet, she cannot move: and she has a blindfolded over her eyes so she cannot see where she might be.

Chapter 13

He whispers you can have it all baby; but first I am going to make you squirm, then I am going to give you something you have never had, before a real man honey; I am going to rock your world for you.

I could hear him grunting and groaning; as I hear, his pants hit the floor.

Then I feel him pulling me to the edge of the table that is when he slams himself into me so hard, I could feel myself shivering with the pain. He knows exactly what he doing to me to hurt me and I do not know why. I cannot figure out what I have ever done to deserve this kind of torturer. He is so brutal, as he slams himself inside of me; repeatedly he bites me on my cheeks I can taste blood. Then he falls on top of me as he comes, all over me.

I feel him slobbering all over me; and the stench was killing me: and I cannot vomit because my mouth taped shut with a ball of some sort and some sort of cloth.

I am thinking how many times will I have to endure this kind of torture.

I believe I passed out: about that time from being so badly tortured, from such an animal: no human being should treat another human being this way.

I am thinking to myself what I ever did to be treated this way. I could feel the sting of tears flowing down my cheeks, and then the dam broke; I could not help crying right out loud, not that anyone cared: I am in big trouble: here and I can't figure my way out of it oh God: how am I going to get out of this mess then, I cried some more.

I screamed to myself please God: keep this evil man away from me; little good my prayers were, because this man had such a sex drive and it seemed he was never satisfied. Each time seemed rougher, than the last: he would bite me and slobber all over me: and hit me as hard as he could, and he did not care where he hit me, as long as it made me cry; out in pain.

I am thinking he is going to kill me: and he is going to enjoy doing just that, I have to get my thoughts to gather, and see if I can out wit him some how?

God please help me I need you now more than ever. How will I ever get to him to take off my restraints?

Then I was thinking: if I could make him think I was enjoying these sex acts; maybe he would let me go: thinking I could do better if I was loose.

I started by getting his attention; by making some loud sounds that is hard when you have a ball in your mouth.

I started bumping my butt up and down on the table. He said if you do not settle down, I am going to use every hole in your body, and I am going to enjoy all of them, so much and the best part will be your pain, which really turns me on more than ever.

I bounced my fanny up and down on the table trying to get his attention, and then he yelled what is your problem bitch? I bounced faster and faster; I needed him to come and take off the gag so, I could convince him that I wanted him.

Boy that made my stomach turn, I hope I can do this; it is going to take everything I have in my power to accomplish this act, and it best be a good one, or I might not make it out of this place alive. I start to moan and try turning my head back and forth, so maybe he will take out the gag; and then I can dicker him: and may be I can convince him: I could be a willing lover; and I will do what ever he wants me to do, but first I would like to clean up for him.

I tell him I really enjoy his love -making, and no one has ever turned me on as he does. All the while I am praying to God; to forgive me for what I am about to do to this man, when I get the chance.

I am trying my hardest to turn him on;

I would just love to clean up for him, which is if that would be all right with him.

Then all I can do is wait: and see what his answer will be. I feel like it is taking him an eternity to answer, then he growls at me: I will let you clean up; before we make love, and you better be as good as you think you are, or I will beat you with an inch of your life.

I hope you understand me: as he growls at me: in a very loud voice, enough to put the scare of God in any human being, I am shaking like a wet dog, I can't seem to stop. I believe he loves tormenting me, and having me terrified of him, that way he can control me. I will make love to you as if you have never had before, that is a promise: and as soon if we can hurry we can get started but I need you to clean yourself up that way we can enjoy each other so much more. Please hurry I need you; I love how you make love to me. I get in the bathroom: and start looking around for anything, I can use to kill this monster.

Then I spot this loose pipe, and I start pulling it back and forth, trying my best to get it loose. I can see it is rusted: I know it won't take much to get it to break loose, after it comes down: I get some soap and start washing, and pulling my fingers threw my hair; to get out all the tangles.

I look into the mirror and my face is swollen, my eyes are black and blue and I have big bite marks on my cheeks. I have choke marks on my neck I know he loves choking me, until I lose consciousness: I cannot believe God would let a man like this live on this earth. I am scared to death: if I fail I know I am going to die right here, and now, I am shaking so bad: I just can't fail. I try talking to my self: God please I need your help now, more so than ever before please be with me in my hour of need. I hear him yelling at me hurry up woman I am getting tired of waiting for you. I scream back at him turn your back to me so you can't see me until I am right in front of you please, you won't be sorry, I promise. I pray he will do as I say, are you ready for me honey. Do you have your back turned? If you are ready, I am on my way out, please answer me, yeah, I am ready: and yes my back is turned so hurry up, I am getting anxious, to taste those lovely lips of yours. I tell my self: you will taste these lips in hell you bastard. When I get my hands on you, I will kill you. I walk out of the bathroom very cautiously; to make sure he has back turned to me. Then I make my move I say hang on darling I am coming I will make all your dreams come true. Then I hit him so hard, blood flew clear across the room, then I hit him repeatedly, I am shaking so hard I drop the pipe. Then I looked for some rope so I could tie him up, and gag him. I know there was some rope around here because he had it to tie me up. I just had to find it. I start going into the other rooms, when I heard him groan. I went back to hit him again even harder this time. I had better hurry before something or someone came around here snooping. I really do not believe: I could go threw this again, I found the rope and some duck tape so I go in to tie his hands, and feet, to gather when he reaches his hand out to grab me, and I hit him again.

I work even faster: then I put the ball in his mouth and run the tape across it twice to make sure he can't get it lose. This is when I spot the hoist in the ceiling, I say to my self I am going to hang this prick; he does not deserve any kind of justice. I found the buttons, that make it go up and down, and I get it down, to where I can fasten it around his neck, then I find a rope to put around his neck, and hooked him up and started the button: to take him up, and I watched him as he squirmed knowing he was about to die.

I cannot even tell you the joy I feel knowing this man will never touch, or harm another human being ever again.

I have to get away from this place, as fast as possible. I do not need someone to catch me here to torture me again. I head toward the trees so they cannot see me. I run as fast I can stay away from all the roads, just in case someone is looking for me. I feel like my lungs are going to burst, but I feel like I cannot quit I know I would not live threw another beating, or to be tortured like I just escaped from, so I had to keep moving.

I am so hungry, and tired, I feel like I am going to pass out, I think to my self: what did I ever do to make God so mad at me, who did I wrong, that I have to pay such a price with my life for. I think, I fell or passed out, I do not know how much time went by, but it was dark outside, when I woke up. I did not even know, what direction, I did not know where I was going so I had better wait until morning. I could tell what direction to go in, then I began to cry, and sobbing so hard, I could not stop myself from shaking. I believe I was going into shock. I had no way of keeping warm. Then it came to me I remembered that leaves give off a heat, so I started gathering up as many, as I could I made a big pile to lay on, then I gathered up a bunch more to lay, on top of my body, and then I was as snug as a bug in a rug.

I fell a sleep and when I woke up, the sun was shinning, on my face and I knew which way I needed to go. I started out slow as my body was so sore, I could hardly move, I guess after the shock wore off, I could feel all the pain in my body. Where it had been so badly torn, used, and beaten. I just hope I can make it home some how, and I can clean my self up; take a nice warm bath: or wait a minute, I best just go to the hospital, and tell them what has happened to me, and get the law involved in this mess: maybe they can figure it out because I sure can not. I guess I am dreaming; because I do not know how far I am from home, and I do not know how, I am going to get their short of any miracles, and I have not been granted to many of them lately.

I know I can't give up; I must keep going some how, I have got to make it back home, after wandering around a while, I hear a noise. I flatten my body down to the ground, and lay as still as a field mouse, being hunted by a fox.

Then I get enough courage to peek up threw the weeds, to see who is out their: and I cannot believe my eyes. A woman and her little girl are picking wild flowers, and I think my luck has just changed for the better.

I get up and I say please do not be afraid, I really need your help, I am in big trouble, and could you please help me? The woman grabbed her little girl, and said woman, just what kind of trouble are you in? I need to get to the hospital I think, I have some broken bones, and I have been brutally raped and bitten, and beaten, please will you help me, and take me to the hospital? I will ask anything else of you, but I really need to get to the hospital.

Okay we will take you and drop you off I do not want to get involved in any of this mess.

Thank you this is all I ask of you, and thank you so much; you have just saved my life.

I just barley remember getting into the door, and I must have passed out, the next thing I remember, is someone asking me if I had been hit by a fright train? I said no I have been raped, and beaten tied down and gagged I have not eaten, or had anything to drink. I really don't know what day it is, I have been wandering, and sleeping, out in the woods until I could see someone, I dared to trust: to bring me to the hospital. Please get a hold of this person for me; he knows whom I am, and what has been going on in my life please. Then they ran the rape kit to see if I was telling the truth, I guess the bruises were not enough for them. Then they got the rape kit back and they said yes, I was differently been raped. I was badly torn. They had given me a shot for lockjaw, and given me a shot to keep me from being pregnant. I guess they had sewed me up and they said the bruises would have to heal them selves.

The next thing I know, I was sleeping and someone was trying to wake me up, Elizabeth honey come on talk to me please. I recognized that voice, and then the floodwaters broke, and all I could do is sob and let go of all the fear, and loneliness, that had been mine, for I do not know how many days. I do not remember how long I have been gone, so please tell me when you last saw me.

Don said it has been three weeks, honey I am so sorry we could not find you, there were no leads, who ever had you covered his trail very well.

I am so happy you were able to escape; I know you must have been living in hell. I am so sorry honey. I hope you will let me help you from now on I do not want to lose you again. Don I can not promise you anything right now, I am in so much pain, I do not know where my life is going and I do not want to hurt you.

Lizzie I am not looking for you to promise me anything, just let me help you, and be with you, till you can figure this thing out, that is all, I am asking of you. Please sweetheart I do not want you to promise me anything...

I am begging you to let me help you that is all, I want All right, Don but remember I promised you nothing, I am having a hard enough time trying to keep my own life straight.

Don I have to confide in you but I need your word you will tell no one this has to be our secret. Can I count on you not to tell anyone and if you can not or would not then please tell me now because this could get you jail time right along with me. I really do not know what I should do confess or plead insanity at the time of my crime. Elizabeth you are a fine lawyer you should know what to do more than I would. Don remembers that was before my amnesia I do not remember any of my life outside of what everyone keeps telling me. I know I should go to the police and explain but I do not know if they will believe me. If only I could just get my memory back I would know what to do. Where is my husband he would be here for me in the hour of my needing him.

Lizzie: I hate to tell you this now but he said he was getting as far away from you as he could to save you, any more problems. He said without him in the picture you would be safer, and no harm will come to you because of him. He said he has caused you so much harm already, and that he has always loved you: and he cannot stand to see you suffer because of him.

I am sorry Lizzie I know you do not want to hear this from me. I said I only want your happiness.

Well mister I know now what I am going to do I am going to the federal bureau of invest ion's I am going to explain what happened to me and what I did to escape with my life, as that man was trying to kill me the slow way with sadistic and inhuman behavior. I had one way out and I took it I could not see leaving him live to get to another woman and to do the same things to her as I had to go threw, so I killed him. Don, if I have to go to prison it will be worth it to me at least I know no other woman will ever have to go threw what I had to. Thank God for that.

Don: would you be so good as to take me to the nearest Federal Bureau of Investigations? I will be in your debt forever for being there for me my friend now we will see how this all will turns out. Don would you please explain to my parents as to what is going on with me and tell them not to worry all will be well.

Chapter 14

After I told, my story to the Federal Ivestigation Bureau They said they have been trying to catch this man for years. They have had undercover agents trying to locate him and have failed. We are so sorry you had to suffer because we have failed in finding this man. Well I guess all we have to do is go and round up the body and have him Identified. Then our records will show that he has met with his maker now that will take. Young woman you have been a very brave and lucky woman to escape with your life. We will have a hearing before a judge. This should not take long after we show our evidence against him and tell how much you had to suffer at the mercy of that man. Please go on with your life we will take care of this situation, if we need you we nowhere we can find you we wish you all the luck in the world.

When I reached my parents home I could hardly control the tears from falling from my eyes it was has if I was a child, wanting my parents to heal my hurt. I know they can only be there for me when I need them and I needed them now more than ever.

I told them what had taken place since he took me against my will, and all I had to endure at the hands of that monster. How I had to trick him in to letting me use the bathroom. I could escape somehow then I started weeping again I hate that memory I just wish I could put it in a bag and throw my memory in the river. The river would carry it into the ocean. I would never have to think about it again. Oh God: will this be possible that I can get on with my life again?

Mom, Dad, do you think I can get on with my life and forget what has happened?

Elizabeth we think you must go to counseling. Then maybe you can get on with a normal life. We think you should go to grief counseling, and get all the help you can, after all dear you have gone threw a lot in this last past year. We think it is best for you and we do not wish to see you go on with all this garbage in your life.

I know Mom, and I will take your advice; because I know that you want me to succeed; and this memory is really taking me down hill. I never thought that anyone person would have to go threw something like this ever. I still wake up in a sweat: I just keep running it around in my mind: I cannot shake it.

I cannot think why anyone could do this to another human being; I scream why God? Would you allow this to go on as long as it did; I just do not understand; honey you never will: this is why we wish you to get into counseling as soon as possible, so please do it first thing in the morning please.

I am going to think positive and I will pray a lot Mom, Dad, as long as I know you are in there backing me up; I know I can do this thing.

Elizabeth have you had any word from your husband? Mom: he told Don, he was getting out of my life because all he has ever done is cause me so much harm.

He said if he was out of my life: I would be safer, well we know how that all turned out. I cannot believe he would just desert me without talking to me about this. I would have respected him more, if he could have brought himself to do this rather, than just run: and leave me alone to fight my own battles. I thought that was what marriage, was about being there for one another: no matter what devil showed his head we could have fought it to gather.

Boy have I ever been disillusioned about this thing called marriage; I thought when we said I do, meant we would stick to gather: through thick, and thin, well if this is what he wants this is what he will get.

Honey: please do not make up you mind, until you get some counseling, and you can get your mind on straight. You have gone threw too much just to make up your mind in the state of health you are in.

Well the very next day: I made my appointment: I do not know if this will be the answer or not. I guess: I will have to start some place so here is as good as any.

When I entered the office; I would rather run then do this but I guess I have to start right here, and right now: if I want to get any better.

When I seen the counselor; all I could think of is, I do not have a long-term memory, just my short term, and it is mostly all bad.

Well then why not start right at the very beginning; of where you can recall.

I told her everything: right from the beginning, she said all right how about we take you back in hypnoses.

I can guarantee no harm will come to you; I will be right here if you can handle the situation.

Now it is up to you: but I think this will help get your memory back. I cannot promise you anything, all I can say is sometimes it does work.

Elizabeth, why not think about it and then get back to me.

I will discuss it with my parents, and then I will get back to you.

When I was going out the door, I saw Donald coming toward me with a big smile on his face. He said hi, beautiful how are you doing I said well, if you want the truth not so hot. Well come with me, and I am going to buy you some lunch, then we can have a down to earth talk how about it?

Don that is the best offer I had all day, he grabbed me by my arm, and pulled me close to him; and said come lets get you fed you have lost a lot of weight; and you can not afford that.

Then the waiter seated us then he brought us the menu, and asked if he could bring us something to drink? Don said please bring us a good bottle of wine, when the waiter came back he poured us each a glass; then he said I will be back in a few moments, that will give you both a chance to look over the menu. We were just sitting: not saying anything. Don finally said Elizabeth; I hope you can feel free to talk to me; I am a good listener.

Don I just feel so deserted; I do not know why; if I have a husband then why is he not here? He should be hereby my side, when I need him the most.

I believe I told you what he told me honey; that is all I know on that subject.

I wish I could help you any other way; I told you I am here for you, if you want me. That is all I can say, now if you wish to talk about any thing else, I am here for you: but I can not help you, as far as your husband, goes; I think he is the most stupid man in the world; to run out on you that way; and I am so sorry honey. I just cannot fix that for you; I wish I could. Shall we order before you go and lose your appetite, and get your self all worked up; over something neither one of us has no control over.

Don, the counselor wants to use hypnotism on me, to see if she can bring back my long-term memory. I told her I would think about it, and discuss it with my parents then I would get back to her.

Why that sounds amazing honey, why would you not want to gain back your memory? Don that is not it at all; I am afraid of what my feelings will be for my husband. Right now I have no feelings, what so ever; and I do not know if I can handle any more trying times. I do not remember what my feeling's are for my husband; and maybe I loved him so much; I let him do as he wishes.

Don, please let us not talk about this any more, I need to relax, for a while. Okay honey what ever you wish is my command. Listen honey; lets go some place where we can dance, and have a few drinks. I don't think it will hurt anything; to just relax for a while and let the world go by what do you think my love?

Oh, I do not suppose it would hurt anything just for a little while, and then when we got to the club the music sounded so sweet. I just started to sway, to the music before we got in the door. We were seated at a table right up front, close to the band. Would this table be to your satisfaction sir? What do you think honey? Yes, it is just fine; I want to hear the music; and dance until the cows come home. Don this is quiets the treat for me; as I have never been in a place like this in my life. I just want to enjoy it all, and you might have to take care of me tonight, are you up for that my friend? I think I can handle one little woman, for one night; if this is what you want. Oh, you bet your sweet ass, this is what I want I want to be blitzed out of my mind: and not have a care in this world.

All right baby: you got it now, let us dance and enjoy the music, as well as the night. Don, you are on, as he danced me around the floor, I felt like a princess: in a fairy tale world; and it felt so good. We danced all night long, and we both broke out in a sweat; but I was not ready to give up, I did not want this night to end, it was one of the few pleasures, I had in my life; and I wanted to enjoy it.

The next morning, or I should say noonday. I was getting sick to my stomach. I could not make it to the bathroom in time so I used the kitchen trashcan. I figured I could take it out and empty it before the day ended if I could survive that long. I made some dry toast, and some black coffee, and went back to bed.

I feel like dying, and I just do not care as of now, this old world has never treated me right from day one, oh well hell there is no use to feeling sorry for my self; it never has gotten me no where.

I need to take care of myself, and get on with it; my husband does not want me then fine: I do not want him either.

This is going to be a new chapter in my book; starting right now, Don wants me then he can have me; I think he is getting bad deal, but he is insisting, on loving me, so I will let him. I will take advantage of that and try loving him back like he wants to. I will be very good to him and hope fully he will not be sorry he met me. I know he will not desert me as if my so-called husband has as a matter of fact he has never been there for me. I should have known he would not make a good husband; or he could have never left me when we were kids without explaining how he felt for me. I was so foolish; to believe he ever loved me; I guess I loved him like a little love struck kid, that never known love. How foolish, can one person be pretty dam stupid; I guess oh well: I need to get on with my life now.

I know Don will always be there for me, he will never leave me as if Alex has that is for damn sure.

I will be seeing my physiologist: maybe we can put our heads to gather and see what we can work out.

I sure have not done so well on my on so far, all I have gotten done is get my self in trouble. Not alone nearly got myself killed; and I had to end up killing some one else on top of that to protect myself.

I hope that my new life will be one hundred percent better; it sure could not be much worse. If this does not work out, I do not know what way I will go from here. I am getting sick of my life, the way it is going now any change will be welcome.

I decided; that I would go a head; with the counselor, and let her hypnotize me, maybe then we can get my life straightened out, hopefully for the better.

I am tired of running around chasing my own tail, and running into dead ends, and detour signs.

I know I have been doing some things right, but also I am doing some things wrong to.

When Alex wanted to take a desk job, I should have insisted on it. I would not have had all these headaches. Then to I would have had him close to me, and not been by myself, all these years.

I have lived like a widow lady, all my married life, the only company I did have was my phantom lover, and he did give me lots of good times, even if they were not real but at least I felt loved.

Well not anymore; I want my life back, and I want it all; I do not want a make believe life. I waited for Alex all my life, and if he can't be there for me now then I guess he never loved me like I loved him. I just cannot wait any longer. I am not going to make any snap decisions until I get my head on straight.

When I got to the physiologist, and told her my decision she was happy that I had made my decision my self. I am glad you are standing up for your self, which is a great beginning. Elizabeth if you are ready let us be getting on with this the sooner we get started, the quicker you get your life back. Elizabeth, I want you to listen to my voice; and you will do just as I say, and remember no one can hurt you; I want you to feel safe, as a baby; in your mother's arms. Now start counting back wards from 100; I will be here for you; when you are asleep listen to my voice; I will tell you what I want you to do.

Now tell me where you are, and what you see after our first session: I already feel like a burden lifted off my shoulder. Sandra said we got a lot done in one session; I believe we can get this thing taken care of faster this way, then if we had not gone along with being hypnotized.

I just want to do what ever it takes, I know it won't happen over night; so I am willing to do what ever you ask of me; I am in your capable hands.

I went home after making my next appointment to rest before I tackle my next problem.

What am I going to do about Don, I really love it that he is there for me, but legally I am still married to Alex.

Oh God is my life ever going to be upside right again, I need your help Lord: I just can't handle all this stress; you said in your word all who are heavy laden, come lay down your load at my feet, and you would take care of them. Father here I am: I need your help desperately; I do not know what way to turn anymore.

After saying my prayer: I feel asleep and there was my phantom lover, waiting for me as usual; I can always count on him; if no one else he always comes to my rescue. I fall into his waiting arms, and he loves me as if no other one could believe me; I do not know what I would do with out him, and his loving.

I think I must have slept for 2 days; or more now I feel like a new woman, and maybe I can figure out what way my life is going.

I just wish Alex had contacted me; I feel like I cannot go into Don's waiting arms without some kind of closure on my old life.

I think I will put in the paper that I am looking for him and see if he will contact me.

If not then I will go on with my life with Don, at least this way I figure I gave Alex the out he must want that he never gave me.

Chapter 15

Don deserves a clean slate, and I really do not want to bring along all my garbage; from my past.

Several weeks later, and I still have not received any kind of message from Alex, so I will go on with my life as planned.

I called Donald, and told him I would like to see him he said he would be right here.

I cleaned my self up, and put on a clean dress, and fixed my hair, and makeup, I wanted to look my best when he see's me.

When Don arrived; he took me in his arms, and whispered in my ear, honey, I have been waiting for this a long time, I have time, and we can go as slow or fast as you wish my darling.

I just want you to care about me, and to give me a chance; to prove my love for you. Just tell me what you want of me, and I will try to give you your every wish. Don; I just want you to know; I will try to give you exactly what you deserve. I know you have been patient with me, and I think you deserve someone better than me; but if this is what you want than you have me.

Don, and I, has been to gather now for a year, and he wants me to set a wedding date.

I do not know why; I just cannot move forward in this relationship; but for his patience, I would be running the other way.

I have been in therapy now for 6 month's and it seems like we have not accomplished a thing. Sharon said we have come along way; but I cannot seem to be able to feel like we have.

I guess; I will have to take her at her word she knows more than I do.

I would like to get back into my law practice but seeing as to how I cannot remember any of my past it probably would do no good and would cause more harm than good.

Don has asked me again can we please get married so we can become as man and wife. Honey I am hurting here I love you so much and I want you to be all mine. Don all right but remember if I get my memory back, I do not know what I will be feeling for any one that is all. I can say on this subject at least you know the truth right? I want you to go in to this with your eyes wide open.

Well Don and I were married on June 14 we just had a small wedding a few friends and relations. We moved into Don's home it was very comfortable and modern he had everything up dated some time ago. Elizabeth I want you to feel at home and just do as you would in your own place so please I hope you can enjoy it here.

Now my darling would you like to go on a honeymoon. I said yes Don could we please let us just get away from here for a while. Well my lovely, where would you like to go? I said how about Hawaii. I have always wanted to go there.

Then that is what we will do; I will make all the arrangements, you relax or maybe you could get things packed up. We can be on our way as soon as I get the transportation taken care of.

I will get the tickets and be right back; I want to sleep in my new wife's arms to night.

When we arrived in Hawaii, it was just beautiful the weather was so nice and warm, people met us with flowers to put around our necks, and did the dance they do for all new comers.

We made our way to the Hotel Don had booked us the bridal suite it was so beautiful I just sat down and cried.

What is the matter darling why are you crying, I am so Happy Don this is beautiful I have never seen anything like it before. Well you deserve it my darling you have been threw so much I just want you to enjoy your self, what ever you want it is my wish. Let us order in to night and then we will see what tomorrow will bring how about that? That sounds good to me we had our dinner with a bottle of champagne I believe the bubble's went right to my head.

Don, I am going to take a nice warm bath please pour me another glass and join me if you wish? When Don came into the bathroom with both glasses, he had stripped of all his clothes.

I said WOW! Don you are really well endowed there big boy.

Elizabeth I just want you to be happy and as you can see I is very happy to have you here with me. I want you so desperately Don you do not have to wait no longer I want you to I can see you are going to make me very happy.

The next day I woke up smiling in my husbands arms, he truly has made me happy. Oh, how he can make love to me with his kisses and love making. I do not think I could be any happier I know I will always have a special place in my heart for Alex but he made the mistake of leaving me when I needed him more than ever in my life.

I guess that old saying is true if you do not take care of your lover someone else will. There will always be some one out there waiting to take care of what you do not. Thank God for small favors or this would be a very sad place to live.

I know it is going to take a lot changes to make adjusting to some one new in my life. I hope Don is willing to help me make the adjustments I know it is not easy even when you love someone, it will take a lot of patience with both of us. I am going to keep seeing my psychoanalyst and I am hoping to get back to my old life style then maybe everything will turn out great. I am not complaining but I really wish to know what it was like to be a famous lawyer that at one time must have been happy with her life style or why else would she lived it the way I hear she did.

Alex was hardly ever around so everyone tells me that I lived alone most of my married life then. Alex divorced me so I went on from there alone. Not asking anyone for anything it sounded like I had it made who would not be happy when living the great dream of a part time wife and a good life as a lawyer.

Well if I ever find out, I will let everyone know it seems as thou everyone is so curious about my life before and after the beating. I lived threw it I guess it is pretty amazing when you do not have to go threw it all, the pain and agony and wondering if you are going to die at the hands of some mad man. I really think God must have been with me and helped me get away other wise I was beyond knowing what was going to become of me. I would be like so many buried out their somewhere and never found. The worst part would be that dirty sick pervert would go on and get some one else to torture.

I am glad he is dead and he never will touch anyone else again, I am happy I at least know that I saved someone else from him.

A person never knows what it is like to be tortured until it happens then some times that is too late. Then you do not get to tell your story. Because you will be dead, and buried somewhere, that no one can find your body. Alternatively, even worse cut up in pieces and scattered all over the country and places that no one ever looks. Believe me it happens to more men and women then anyone knows or even cares about. How about the homeless; who keeps track of all of them. No one even cares as long as do not bothered with him or her.

Well I am here to tell you it is not a good thing to happen to anyone. It is to bad all the bad people could not put away. Where could they not hurt anyone else? Then the world would be safer place to live, but we all know that is a fantasy.

When I get better and I get my brain back to where it is supposed to be I am going to do my best to get some of these sick men and women off the streets.

For good especially them perverts that are out there harming the little children of our beautiful country.

I think this irks me more than anything some one taking advantage of innocent little children that cannot take care of them selves.

If all goes well and I can have Gods blessings this will all happen I will not go back on my word.

When Donald gets home, I am going to tell him about my day and listen to him. Where he is working now and how he can afford all these nice things.

He must have a very good job that is all I can say, I am not complaining that is for sure.

When I went to my place, I know my stuff was nowhere as nice as his was so we gave all my stuff to the Salvation Army.

I know they do good work and help many people and they can use all the help they can get.

I fixed a nice dinner, put some candles on the table and opened a bottle of wine from his wine refrigerator.

I took a long and leisurely bath, and then I fixed my hair so I felt like a new person and I did not look to bad either.

When I heard Don I ran out to meet him and welcome him home, when I reached the door, I sensed that Donald must have had a bad day and he was wearing it on his face. I asked him what was wrong. He just said nothing for me to be concerned about. I said Don I am your wife please do not exclude me from what is bothering you.

I know I might not be able to help you but you can use me as a sounding board. I am willing so what is the problem and if you think you are going to cut me out of your life think again because I will not live like that. Donald do you understand me?

Elizabeth I do not want to burden you with my problems so please let us just have a nice dinner and wind down a little. I will see how I feel after my belly has been filled. If I am lucky maybe, I can make love to my beautiful wife when we are finished with our dinner.

Don I will be so happy when I can get back to work I am not used to sitting around all day with nothing to do.

Liz I want you to be happy and I wish you could be happy here taking care of me and our home and maybe we can work on having a family some day. Don you know I cannot have children, and even if I could, I am not so sure I want any children! I have to be very sure of this before I even want to discuses it.

This world is not a very nice place to live in I would not want to bring a child in it just so some pervert could mess it's life up for them no thank you I will not do this.

Don please lets not even go in that direction please, I want to help you anyway I can and this is not the direction I am willing to take so let's just drop this subject okay.

After we had our little discussion, we settled in the living room to relax while I try to pry more information out of Don.

As usual, he clamed up and remained tight-lipped and no matter what I did, he would not discuss anything about his day. I went and put my arms around his neck and said all right honey lets go to bed and try to forget this day.

I knew this was all he was waiting for and he was ready in all the ways that was important.

After wards, we just snuggled and he gave me a nice back rub with something that must have tasted good because he was nibbling on other parts of my anatomy. I found out right at the beginning of our relationship that he had a healthy sexual appetite so I was not surprised.

Don now that you are all relaxed would you like to discuss anything with me. Don if this is the problem than I will shut up and leave you alone. Liz if I want to discuss something with you I will do it without you questioning me at every move I make. Honey it is all work related and does not have anything to do with you. If it did, I would say it did so let drop the subject before some one gets angry and that someone is not me.

Liz lets get some sleep, and from now on, you play at being a little woman of the house. In addition, take care of my needs for as long as I have you. When you get back to work we will make some other arrangements. Maybe hire someone to keep the house and cook the meals I no you will be to tired.

As time went on Don continued to grow further and further away, I tried, time, and time again to reach out to him but he was like a man possessed.

I just went on with my life as if I knew what was going on. I went to all my meetings came home and fixed the meals and kept the house like someone cared besides me.

I may as well of been single because I had no one to talk to and I was feeling very lonely again. I decided to talk with my mother I needed to talk with someone. I feel like I am going crazy and as usual no one cared, this is as bad as it can get I might as well be living in my own apartment.

When I reached my mother's she was busy in the garden I said Mom do you have time to visit I need to talk with you I have a problem and I do not know what to do about it.

Please help me I am feeling so lonely I am not happy in this marriage I am more alone now than ever Don will not talk to me and he is so with drawn I cannot reach him I have tried my best over and over again.

What can I do? I thought about leaving him but he said if I ever leave him, he would kill me. Mom helps me decide what to do Liz you are a big girl I cannot tell you what to do.

Get a hobby or volunteer at the hospital or at the humane shelter they need help all the time.

You just have to much time on your hands and that is not good because you are over thinking everything and you imagination is running away with you have to keep busy then everything will be alright. I would not lead you astray. Thanks Mom I will do just as you told me and I will keep myself busy. I have faith in you my daughter you are a very good girl and I know you can do it. Liz if you need to talk again just let me know I am here for you and ask them if they need some help. The animals the girl I talked to said I am sure we do but you will have to talk to Gloria she is the one that takes care of this kind of thing my name is Audrey. I am so happy to meet you and if you need any thing just look me up I am here most all the time. When we got to where this person named Gloria was she reached out, and took my hand, and said I am happy to meet you. In addition, if you are looking for work and your not squeamish we have some jobs for you.

If you would not mind, we could use some one to walk the dogs they are getting antsy. Then when you get back, we will tell you what else needs done, and believe me there is plenty to be done. I hope you do not wear out to fast we really need some good help around here. We have had our share of those that like to hang out but do not get much work done. Welcome and good luck we will be seeing you at the lunch break. Audrey you fill her in and take some information from her and show her where the lunchroom is and where the restroom is.

I walked the dogs and cleaned some cages, and gives some bathes to the dirty little ones that an older woman dropped them off. She said she could not take care of them or feed them. Today they were so skinny and filthy. I cannot believe how people treat animals and one another I am sure God did not have this in his mind when he formed our big wonderful world we live in. But I guess some people just do not have any pride in themselves or others all they do is tare up and destroy and kill a there is a lot of sick people in this world. I cannot believe how many there really is living here and causing a lot of pain and misery for Gods innocent little children, and animals and not alone some adults suffer at there hands.

I do not want to think about this any more I hate these thoughts, they just creep in any time I let my guard down.

When I left that night my butt was dragging, Don had to be there when I got home now I will have to explain where I have been.

I went in to start fixing some dinner but Don grabbed my hand and swung me around to face him and asked me where in the hell have you been have you been out whoring around? I have been volunteering at the human shelter they need the help, and I need something to keep me busy. About that time Don Hit me right across the face. I will have you know I will not have my wife working out side the home you can find enough to do around here to keep you busy. I never want to hear about this again this subject is closed. Now get in there and fix me a nice dinner.

I grabbed a poker and smashed it against his head he went down like a ton of lard. I tied his hand and feet, and pulled him into the kitchen and let him lay on the floor like the animal he was. You want dinner I will feed you like the dogs eat and you don't even deserve that much and when you have had enough you let me know and I will call the police and they can come and take you away because I am not going to live like this. I have had my share of ugly mean men like you and I will not stand for this kind of abuse from you nor any one else. After a few days of me treating him like a dog and I got my things packed up. I was ready to leave and after I am gone I will press charges against him and have the police go and have him arrested and put into jail. From there on I will live by my self I will never trust another man as long as I live.

I know the way it is turning out I might not be around for long but I will go down fighting.

It seems I am in this world alone, and I sure can't trust no one person to be there for me. Well that is just fine I will do this my self from now on, I went back to the shelter and was cleaning the kennel when this beautiful dog left in a cage he was beaten and dirty the poor little fellow looked so bad he could hardly stand up by him self. I rushed over to his side and helped him to the table so the Dr. could clean him up I never left his side from the time he was brought in to the time he had been taken care of and put in the cage. Every day I took care of him and as he got better I asked if I could take him home and care for him. When he was able to be adopted I wanted to adopt him I want him for my own.

I could identify with that dog as I too had beaten down just like him we are two of a kind. I will protect him and he will protect me we have become fast friends and we love one another. I took him with me every day and walked him along with the other dogs he got along with them very well I did not have any problems with any of them. I think them all new I loved them all; I put my heart and soul in to these poor animals. They were just innocent by standers that some evil person took out his anger on some one that could not fight back.

I will fight for these animal rights if no one else will, I will get some money put to gather and I will help them as much as I can.

Well when I was on my way home, we were walking down the side street when some one grabbed me. The next thing I knew I was in the hospital and I was suffering from a concussion. I had been hit me on the head, and they stole my purse. I am thinking it does not pay me to leave my Condo. One good thing came from that I did get my memory back. I now can get back to being at being a lawyer and making good living and try to start my new life over again as soon as I get my divorce.

I can grant you one thing it will be a long time before I marry another man I am threw with men. I decided that I would to go threw all the classes. I do not want to suffer at the hands so some mad man again.

I just hate having to leave my dog alone but I made sure to have a young man take her for some walks along with the other dogs he walks.

Chapter 16

love him and I want the best for him I feel he has suffered enough at the hands of a human, if you would call them that.

My first case was a breeze; I guess my co-workers are taking it easy on me knowing what has happened to me. I will have to prove my self-worthy all over again, but that is all right with me I can handle it. These partners have always understood animals they do not treat people bad. But it is people that treat animals badly I hate knowing men will beat on some one that can't fight back.

Well I hope someday I can face these kinds of men in court. I will do my very best to see they get some hard time out of it and not just a fine.

I went in to speak with the lawyers that I had been working with to see if I could get back in with them. They all were so happy to see me we were all smiling and hugging each other and everyone was trying to speak at the same time.

I was so happy to be back with all my friends, and able to get a new start in my life. I think this will be a piece of cake.

After I got my divorce, I was so happy to have that taken care of and from now on, I will carry a gun and some hornet spray in my bag anyone trying to hurt me will suffer dearly. I will shoot first and ask guest ions later. I went to the firing range and took lessons. Then I went to get some pointers on how to protect myself. I found this to be very interesting and I enjoyed it so much I put it behind me and been there for me Thank God for them.

I will not let them down I will work very hard to prove to them that Ian not going to let them down.

I decided to have my town house re furbished and I had a designer come and work things out so it would be right.

I had a very little in put but I told her exactly what I wanted and if I was not satisfied she would do it over again the way I want it at her expense I do not believe you can beat that kind of a deal right?

I went to spend some time with my parents while they took over my place, and part of the deal is to make a special place for my dog. I want her to be happy to so that was part of the plan.

Things were going so nicely and we were very happy my life was going according to my plans. My parents was happy to have me back home for a while and they both enjoyed Pepper my dog. That made me happy that she just made there home her home. My Dad took her for some walks, and he bought her some special treats, plus she got a few table scrapes and she really loved that. She was my sweet heart I put all my love on her and she deserved it I wish to make her as happy as possible. Well it took a few weeks and then I got the call they were finished with my place townhouse. Wanted me to come to see if I could live here in my new home and be happy with it. When I entered my home, I was flabbergasted it was beautiful. Each and everything was just beautiful, and exactly the way I wanted it. I told them thank you all so very much for doing such a great job I am so happy with all of it. I can hardly wait to get back here and make it my own it is going to be just great. W e wiped out all the old memories and now I am going to begin my life all a new, no worse memories. I am still seeing my counselor at least once a week until she says she is happy with me. How well I am doing.

I went home and put on some romantically music and just danced with my self while sipping some champagne. Then the doorbell rang and I stopped with a jerk because I was not expecting anyone. I took my gun, hid it behind my back, and looked out the peephole. I did not recognize the man outside my door so I said may I help you young man? He answered me with I have some flowers here for you, I said place them by the door and leave with this he said but you need to sign. I will tell you what you slide it under the door and I will sign and send it back to you other wise you may take them flowers right back where they came from do you understand me? So he did as I told him after a while I opened the door just long enough to get the flowers I could not think of who would be sending me flowers. Now who would waste money on buying me flowers?

I just sat and looked at them flowers they were beautiful. I waited until after my dinner to look at the name on the flowers, I did not want to have my dinner ruined.

I worked up the nerve to see who they were from and I would never guess who sent them of course it was Alex of all people I could not believe my eyes now after all this now he sends me flowers I can not believe this.

I lay a wake for hours while my thoughts ran rampant in my mind, and then came the tears for my lost lover. I know this sounds silly but Alex was my first and my childhood sweetheart. I had only loved him from the start and then he deserted me. When I needed him in my life, the most of all he just cut and ran with out any kind of explanation.

I know I should just forget him but since I got my memory back, I cannot quit thinking about him. I hate my self that I am so weak to let him take over all my thoughts but I cannot think of anything that will chase him from my thoughts.

I really need some sleep; I have a big case ahead of me tomorrow I have to be a best. I got up and got a cup of hot coco and a couple of aspirin maybe then I can rest. My head hit the pillow and I was asleep and dreaming of my lover he was waiting and beckoning me to himself. I was in his arms and he was kissing me and touching me all over. Then he took my breasts in his mouth and suckles them like a hungry babe he was driving me crazy. Then he entered me with a hard push then he waited all the while he is kissing my neck and my mouth hungrily I cannot wait for him to continue my body wants him.

I am shaking with dispassion of what he may do next that is when he began to take me all the way home. I am thinking to my self I really needed this my feeling have been so pent up I feel like a high strung violin and then he gave me that finishing push over the edge and I scream out with sure delight as my body quivered with satisfaction.

The next day I feel like a spring chicken my body is so relaxed, I feel like I could swim the English Channel with out stopping.

I entered the office and everyone looked at me and said you look just great what have you done to your self? I just got a good restful sleep that I needed badly I feel more relaxed now than I have for a very long time.

I am ready to get this case on the road; I have been reading and studying this case for a couple of weeks now. I have been talking with the client and taking notes, and I even hired an investigator to check out his wear a bouts and into the wear a bouts on the evening of the crime.

I gathered up all the paper work on this case and I almost got out the door when I ran smack tab into Alex.

I just stood and stared at him at first then he really pissed me off H e was so bold as to ask me how I am as if he really cared. I said I could not see as if it is any concern of yours Alex. Now if you do not mind I have some business I have to take care of so please step away.

Elizabeth please will you take some time for me I am begging you. I would like to make my self perfectly clear to you Alex. When I needed, you the most you just cut and ran so as far as I am concerned you can keep on running. I do not need some one as you to mess me up again so put that in your pipe and smoke it this is my final wish now sir step back I am a busy woman.

I was shaking so bad I thought I would fall over, but I maintained my balance and walked away with my head held up straight.

I did this and I could not believe I had the strength to stand up to the one man that had meant so much to me all of my life.

I had a hard time trying to concentrate on my case my mind kept trailing back to Alex. I told myself to wake up and pay attention I really need this case to go as planned. My co- workers were depending on me as well as our client I had to put my thoughts on hold and get through this.

I know I can do this I need to get my priorities straight I am a better person than this to let Alex get to me again.

I did a good job on this case and all my co- workers were waiting for me to congratulate me. They had a party all set up seeing to how it was the weekend they decided I needed a party. I did not know how to thank all of them so I just said it the best way I knew how. I told them I was so happy to be back at work and thanked them for believing in me when I did not even know what I was going to do if they had not. I am so thankful for all of you this job means more to me than you all will ever know. So all I can say is thank you all so very much now let's get this party on the road.

We partied until the early morning hours; and you all know it has been so long since I have been so happy. However, if I get any happier I will be sick all day tomorrow and I do not want that. I will say my good byes and I will see you all Monday morning and thank you all again.

I went home and set out to take care of my dog and give her some attention that he really deserved. I talked to him as if he could understand me, and told him.

Chapter 17

About my day as I brush his little body. Pet him, and told him how much I loved him then we headed for the bedroom as she sleeps at the foot of my bed.

I heard a noise and so did pepper he turned his ears up and turned her head back and forth as if waiting to see if she could hear it again.

Then there was a knock on the door. I could not believe someone would be knocking at this very early time of the morning.

I said who is there. I heard a voice saying Lizzie please let me in I need to explain some things to you. Please give me the good courtesy to listen to what I have to say. Then if you wish, I will not bother you again, Oh if only I could believe that. Alex you might try talk*ing to me at a descent hour of the day. Right now, I am too tired too even think straight so please call me tomorrow. I will try to squeeze you in my busy schedule you know how important you are as a man.*

The next day my Mother called before I even got out of bed and asked me to come over for lunch. I said all right seeing as to how she rarely asks me for anything.

When I arrived I could feel like something was wrong but I do not know exactly what it could be. I went in and hollered out to my Mother where you are Mom? She yelled back I am in the kitchen my dear come on in.

There he was sitting at the table big as you please as if he was the most important person in the world. I said what kind of arrangement is this any way my own Mother taking sides against me her own Daughter.

Listen to him Liz that is all I ask of you please. All right, go for it Alex seeing as to how important this seems to be to the both of you I is listening.

The only reason I left you was for your own good it seemed like all I was doing was causing you a lot of harm. Did your friend tell you what I said? I love you Lizzie, and I always have it about killed me when I heard you had married Donald. So I stayed away I know you think the worst of me. I am so sorry for all the pain you have had to endure, so I have been working at a desk job now for the last past year. I just want you to hear my side of things as it seems Mr. Donald forgot to say anything and you have been thinking the worst of me. I only ask that you think about this and get back to me please. I said I would think about it and I was out the door in a shot if I did not I am afraid I would break down right there in front of him and my Mother. I do not exactly know what I was feeling as of right now I just felt nothing.

When I got home, I did not know what I would do but as of right now, I was going to run with my dog.

I reached the door and said come on pepper we are going for a run I need to get some of my thoughts straight.

After a while, we stopped and I went over to have a seat on the a bench, and was talking to pepper, and telling him all about what had taken place, and then I broke down and started to cry my heart out. All right pepper, we are going to stay busy with work, and volunteering at the Humane Society. You can come with me as much as time will allow, or I will see you are taken care of I love you pepper. I kept my nose to the grindstone, and when I was not sleeping, I was at work, and working very hard. I did not want to think about Alex or any other man I have had my fill of them all. I know you are to forgive and love one another. I am not ready to do this as of yet I think this will take time and maybe it will never happen I have no idea what I might be feeling a year from now or a month from now. Time has gone by and I am working very hard at the office, and at the Humane Shelter. I love working with the animals they give you so much love and they do not expect any thing back. I like taking them on their walks this way I can take my pepper along for a walk. He really loves that he walks so very proud when he turns walks as if he is some kind of royalty. He thinks he is a leader of the pack even if he is little he is a tough little puppy and he has a bad time of it in his little life.

I like to bath them and give them clean safe place to live in there own kennels.

I will try my best to care for all of them and see that they get good homes and I will check on them to make sure they are safe even after they do have a good home. You just cannot be to sure about people they may start out with good intentions but sometimes they go a little different after a while. Then they feel like they are too proud to bring them back to the shelter. That makes them feel like a failure to do has they had promised. Well I will be checking on all of them I have the paper work on each and everyone adopted, and believe me I am going out to check on them. While I am doing my job, I have met nice people, and I have even talked some of them in to coming to the shelter to work with some of the animals. I am so proud of these people my heart really goes out to them. Some of them even bring there children so they will know how to treat these poor neglected animals. These Children are so kind to the animals it feels like there little hearts goes out to some of them neglected animals. They just curl up in there little arms, and wait to be loved they hug, and kiss them as if they were there very own babies. I have had more adoptions than even I can believe. They give me a brand new car to check up on the animals. One of the women that work with us her husband owns an automobile shop. She convinced her husband to donate the brand new car. She even talked him in to the care of the car right along with the car. We said we would advertise for him seeing as to how he done us such a big donation.

We had a magnetized sign made to put on the door that said this car donated to the humane shelter for the good of the animals. Then we had the name of the dealership along with the humane shelter. He certainly deserved that much and more.

Chapter 18

One day as I walked into the shelter there stood Alex strong and tall as always. Even as handsome as he has always been, my heart just started pumping so fast I thought I would pass out. I walked up to him and asked him what he was doing here? He said I have come to adopt a dog I need one for some companionship I do get a little lonely living all alone in that big house. I did not know you owned a house when did all this happen? I bought it when I first come back to see if we could work things out after I explain to you what had happened. I wish you would give me another chance honey. I will do my very best to make you happy, and to protect you from that entire cruel world out there. I took a nice desk job, and no one is after me and we can be happy, and have a good family life. Lizzie please lets try this one more time I love you so much. I have always been so miserable with out you; I have been in a living hell. Please have some dinner and talk about this please. All right Alex but I am not making any promises, I want a chance to tell you all about what I have been through, and if this is all right with you. I am going to give you one more chance. Honey I will pick you up at 6:00 pm so be ready my darling. Well when Alex picked me up, he was driving a brand new Mercedes Benz convertible it was just beautiful. I looked at Alex and lost my breath he was right down handsome with his sport coat, and them beautiful eyes burning into me. I believe he had already undressed me with his eyes. I had to blush a little, and I could feel the burn clear down to my shoes. Oh, my God he can still steal my breath away with just one look.

How am I going to keep my hands off him, I took the seat next to him, and I could feel his hot body next to me. Then he handed me a big box of chocolate's, and one big red rose I laid them down next to me in the seat I said where are we going Alex? I thought we would go to my house, I have dinner all fixed with a bottle of Champagne chilling just for you my love. Well I suppose that is all right but no funny business, and I mean that. This will be a very business like dinner where we can talk to one another, and see where we stand.

I could not even begin to tell you how I felt about Alex; He was turning me on without even trying. W hat am I doing here I do not want the feelings I want to hate him, and I cannot work past wanting him my body was betraying me. He has always been able to turn me on. That has not changed one little bit

Alex is trying to talk to me but his voice is quivering, and he was a little horse. I was trying to listen to what he was saying but my mind was roaming to other areas of his antimony. I know what he was feeling because we always had a very good sexual life we both had good sexual appetite for one another.

He came over to me, and I sucked in my breath, I could not breathe he pulled me up into his arms, and I let him kiss me. I just melted into his arms I could not help myself I was like putty in his hands.

Alex made passionate love to me kissing my body, my breasts as he suckled them like a little baby I did not want him to stop he could have made love to me all night long, and I would not have stopped him. I wanted it all I wanted him inside me all 12 inches of him working me into lather, as we both sweat as we were in a sweat shop. I screamed with all the passion I could work up I wanted him to make love to me all night long I could not get enough of him. I was like a starved orphan I did not want to give him up I wanted more oh honey I have missed you so much please don't leave me again.

Never my darling, I have always loved you from the time we were little children, and I never quit. I know I have always caused you a lot of pain but never again. I will make it up to you honey, please let me try. Then he made love to me again but more of a slower, and deeper than the first time. It was even more enduring as he filled me up I screamed with so much joy in my life. I used my nails on his back I know I must have left long marks. I needed him in me over, and over I cannot quit I want him inside me forever.

I want his love more than food or water or the air I breathe I need Alex he is my life.

After making love, so many times I lost count I lay in his arms and enjoyed all of him. But at the same time it can cause you so much pain used in the wrong way in the wrong hands of some abnormal manic.

He said please do not quit I love your mouth on me it about drives me crazy. Boy oh boy does he know how, and where to touch me with his mouth his breath is so hot it really turns me on I love that heat from his breath, and hot tongue. I think we need some time alone just the two of us so we could make up for lost time. I just cannot give him up right now I want him more than life itself. Lord help me for being so weak in the flesh.

When I am away from Alex during my working hour's I have a hard time to keep him in the back of my mind.

I really need to keep my mind on my work, these people pay good money to have us fight for there rights so we need to win our cases.

There is a time, and a place for everything and I need to get my priorities straight.

I know we cannot be to gather all the time and I do not know where our love will take us. Because we have had to go through so much right from the first time I met Alex I knew I would always love him. I never thought anything would come of it but it certainly was something I wanted and never thought I would have a chance with him. I always thought he only seen me as a little sister type. Boy was I wrong and we have had our share of hard times but it always brings us even closer than before.

Chapter 19

Little did I know what was in store for us I could never have guessed in a million years?

I thought Don was still in prison but guess what, and who showed up again in my life.

It started with messages and flowers coming to my office signed a secret admirer. I did not think to much about it at first, and just dismissed it, and laughed about it. I told Alex about it, and he said be careful honey this person could be some wacko you could not be too careful. Especially after all you have been through so please be extra alert where ever you go please try to keep some one with you at all the time.

With my work, I am always out amongst all types of people, and I do not get to pick, and choose.

I was to meet with one of my clients, and we agreed to meet at his favorite restaurant. I was not concerned at all the day was beautiful, and I was so happy to be alive, and in love with my soul mate. How many people can say that I never thought I would be saying anything like this in a million years? I just thought my days of happiness were at, and end, I would be alone for the rest of my life.

We never know what God has in mind for us, no matter what we think he has his own version of what he wants for us.

Our meeting went very good, and we had drawn up some plans that needed to my immediate attention. I was on my way back to my office when I felt something strange. I just had a cold chill go down my back

I knew something was wrong. I got my phone, and called my office and told them something was wrong. Please have some one come, and meet me please, I know it did not take them long, and they were there escorting me back safe, and sound.

That is when I said I need someone to have my back when I have to be away from the office. I cannot go through any more bad times like that I have already been there and done that and I am not eager to do it all over again.

Therefore, I hope you can see my point of view. I hired my self a private eye, and I expect him to take care of me, and to know what is wrong before it actually happens. I am dead serious I am not ready to have to be tortured again not in this lifetime.

Alex agreed with me that really made me happy, I want this man to be apart of my life but I need to be true to my self. I feel like I cannot truly trust anyone with my life. And I know it will take some time before I can truly trust a man again with my feelings.

I know many people act as if they do not care about or even talk about sex. I grew up in that kind of atmosphere in fact no one talked to each other about any thing. I really hated that the grown ups thought we did not have a need for good advise or bad. I always thought, and felt alone, and unloved and something was missing from my life. I never knew how to relate to others out side of my sibling is because they are the ones that took care of most of my needs.

Sure, the parents made the money, bought the food, and paid the bills but that was the limit to what they did for us. I guess what ever you needed you had to guess at it or learn by trial and error well I certainly learned things the hard way and it certainly was by trial and error and believe me it has been at my own expense. I have suffered dearly for my insufficient knowledge. I will have enough knowledge to know the difference between love, and lust. I will have enough to get me through with out all the pain that goes with it. I know people say life is a learning tool, and Mother Nature will put you in many classrooms of knowledge, and you should learn something new everyday.

Some people are lucky, and have parent's that are involved in there lives, and helping them with everyday problems. While other children grow up alone, and have to learn things the hard way on the streets, and by doing like I said by trial and error. Then to many of the times even with there a life it is sad but true, to know one person has it truly made in this big wonderful world we live in. If others would tell of there, heartache's and problems there would be so many books out there no one could read them all. If we only had the time and money to listen to even a few stories and I know there would not be any to stories that would be alike.

I know in my line of work you hear a lot of what happens to some one when know one seems to care. Then some times some people care to much and go over board the other way and try to buy there children's love. Some children do not have any rules to go by and grow up doing whatever feels good. S o if anyone really knows the right way of bringing up a family I wish I knew what it might be. I guess life has no good rule book even preacher's children grow up and do the wrong things, and go on that crooked path I certainly wish I knew what the answer would be Then maybe I could write a book on it.

All I can honestly say is that when I love my man, and he loves me there is no greater thing than the love we have for one another. I believe everyone has sex, and use sex in some way. I have not done this, but when I have been married, I enjoy our sex life with every bone in my body, and I do not think it nasty or dirty. I get a some comments on how can you feel so free to talk about sex as you do. Therefore, I think to myself people think sex is dirty and nasty. I feel for these people because I know sex is healthy and enjoyable. Unless someone pushes it on you, I am sorry to get of the subject but like I said when I am away from my love I am thinking about him all the time. I have been through some really bad, and I do not wish to do it all over again

Chapter 20

This is why I am planning on running for State Prosecutor I do not care what I have to do I am running. I have the Education, and the experience to win now all I have to do is start promoting, and campaign in full force. I want to be the one to send some of these criminals where they belong I will have my man Friday to help me to do the investigating.

I believe I know enough people, and with my husband by my side, and with his friends we can win this thing.

When I told Alex about my plan he said honey I know I have done you wrong all these years but if you are sure this is what you wish to do I am with you all the way.

I just hope you know your life will be in more danger now then ever before. I will do what ever you need me to do.

Alex there is one big thing I need to take care of I need you to go undercover to help me get rid of one big hurdle before this thing can take place. I told Alex my plan he agreed and was more than ready to help me. I went on with my business as usual. I had my bodyguard working closely with me on a case that I really needed to win. We were out investigating the stories, we needed to see if they had been fabricated. Well everything seemed to check out just the way he had said it would. It took us just a few days to round up some witnesses and mean time we needed a break so I suggested a place for us to eat. I really felt like celebrating so we went to this nice restaurant. I wanted some champagne and a nice meal this was the place to get both.

We were half way through our meal and the hair on my back stood up on end I was trying to be very cautious but I knew something was wrong. Then there he was twice as nasty as I remembered him he was unshaven, and very rugged looking like he was a tramp on the street or even worse I believe he was schizophrenic. His eyes had that glassy crazy look he scared me just looking at him. I had no idea he would actual show up in person in a public place like this but here he was. Twice as nasty, and more intimidating than before I could feel my body starting to shake I could not stop, I was safe enough but I also knew this man was ruthless. I held my breath while waiting for him to make his move, and believe me it did not take him long. He had reached out, and grabbed the plate we had been eating of, and threw it in the face of my body guard. Then he had pulled his gun, and threatened everyone to stay out of the way or he would shoot him or her, and me. He was shouting, and almost in a hysterical voice, he was looking right at my bodyguard and said she is mine, and you will never have her do you understand me. I will kill her, and I before you or anyone else can have her. Now come on we are leaving he had me by the arm, and was twisting it behind my back. We were headed out the door when all of a sudden I seen a flash, and then I was knocked to the floor. It all happened so fast, I did not have anytime to react. Then there was my handsome husband he swung in the door about the time were headed threw. Alex, caught Don with a big surprise fist to the face, and knocked him out cold. I was so happy to see Alex I just started crying Alex pulled me into his big arms, and whispered in my ear now honey we can't have the future prosecutor crying now can we?

Well honey I guess we took care of that problem, and if you ever need me for anything all you have to do is whistle. Alex I will do more than whistle, come here you I grabbed him around the neck, and kissed him a sweet, and loving kiss with more to come later. Alex took me in his arms, and said I cannot wait I need your loving all of it forever. Please Elizabeth marry me again and I will always be there for you. I promise you I will never do anything with out consulting you first. Alex I feel we have grown a lot with the years so yes I will marry you only with the understanding that you will not interfere with my job, and how I do it. Honey that will be easy compared to all we have been through in our lifetime.

I had Alex start his campaigning for me, I had him order buttons, and billboards, and we needed a building and workers to operate the phones. I know he had many of his friends to help in there spare time. I needed to speak with the lawyers and explain to them what I am going to do. I hope they will understand that I need to do this for me and all the other victims in this world. I told Alex I really need his help to see everything gets done and gets done the right way. Elizabeth when are we going to take time to get married? Alex how about this weekend, we can fly to La Vegas and enjoy our weekend and get married. I love that idea that sounds like we can enjoy our selves and take in a few shows, and make love, eat gamble a little I love that idea.

The next day I went straight into the office, I said to my coworkers I explained I needed to call for a board meeting. When we all were to gather I began explaining what I wanted to do. When I was threw explaining they were all so happy for me, and wished me good luck. Then they said they would be there for me, and they would help anyway they could. I will really appreciate that I know this will leave you shorthanded but I will stay until you can replace me.

When I got home, Alex was on the phone he gestured for me to come over. I sat down and waited for him to hang up the phone.

Honey I have made reservations for us at the hotel, and our flight would be that night can you be ready by then. Yes, I can my darling I can start packing right now. How about you will you be ready? I am ready I bought you some gifts when we get to the hotel you can have them.

I can only say I am the luckiest woman alive to have another chance to have a loving man in my life. I am lucky to have my soul mate, as well as my childhood sweetheart. I know Alex will always be there for me now; we have both been threw so much in our lifetime. Like I said, life will teach you many things maybe not all good but I guess it is something we need to know. I now realize God did not promise us a rose garden. I do not pretend to know why we all have to go threw the bad as well as the good. I only know what I have learned if it does not kill you, it will make you stronger. If life gives you lemons all you can do is make lemonade. I will try my best to do a good job, as well as to be a good wife. I want my husband to be as happy with me as I am with him. I know he can make me happy, I have always been in love with Alex, and I believe he has always loved me. Sometimes circumstances gets in between us, and we all have made some kind of mistakes. I know I am not perfect and never will be but I will try my best to help those who are less fortunate than we are. I will still be there for those poor animals, that are being abused as well as for the people that are being abused or mistreated. I want justice for us all I will give it my best shot.

Right now, I am going to give my new husband all my attention; I can only be in one place at one time. When I am with my husband, I will give him my all. When I am on the job, I will do everything I can to uphold the law. I will prosecute the criminals fully that the law will allow.

So right now I am lying in this sweet man's arms, he is doing his best to turn me on. My mind has been a million miles away, well that will end right now. I look at him, and smiled well honey here we are again I hope for this will be the last time at least for us getting married. We can always come back for a second honeymoon. Come here you, and let us make mad passionate love I said this will be my pleasure. He kissed me with all the pent up feelings that he has had all these years. He about blew my socks off Alex I love you so very much. Then he took me with everything he could muster up. He just took my breath away I feel limp into his hot sweaty hard body. Honey you do that so very well, I could do this all night of course with a couple of breaks in between.

Sir I think that certainly could happen. I called room service and told them we need a fruit platter with caviar and champagne. Yes, ma'am we will bring it right up with our compliance for your wedding present.

After we had some food and we bathed each other, and gave each other a good massage with hot oil, that made you feel like a new person. That way we can begin again in our love making I know one thing for sure if there is anyone thing some one can do good. Alex does not need any lessons on this subject his lovemaking is just wonderful, and exciting. Alex knows every move that turns me on and then he can turn me off and get me to the point that works me right back into wanting him again. I just hang on for dear life I feel like he sucks me right into himself all. I can do to keep from losing my mind is scream with sure delight I shiver with so much excitement the sweat is flowing between us down his hairy chest into his crowning manhood. Our bodies are weak from the pleasure we have just shared. Alex I just do not understand how our lovemaking can keep improving. It just seems terrific then again, it seams even better the more we do it. I just wonder how much better it can get without us going crazy oh my God that is so good then he pulls me into his hot sweaty body, and kisses me so passionately I just don't know how I can stand all this love making. When we have to leave, I am going to miss this so much. I know when we are home things are going to get so hectic.

I want us to be able to make love all the time, Honey I hope you will not let me go without making love to me. Lizzie lets set the clock early enough so we have time for each other before we have to deal with the public. Alex that is the best idea you have had yet I love that idea. Come here my little minx, I have been without you far to long and it liked to drive me crazy. I never want to go threw that ever again. Li z you are the best thing that has ever happened to me I love you so much. You are so beautiful honey, you just make me weak in the knees. When I watch you I could not believe that I could have had you all to my self all these years. I have wasted so much time I need by butt kicked that is so sad. Elizabeth can you ever forgive me for wasting so much time I know it was my entire fault but when you are young, you just do not think about these things. I just thought about my job and trying to make a better place for us to live in.

Alex I know I never thought about anything else either, I just thought we would always be to gather. I never once thought about all the problems that we have encountered. I do believe it all happened for a reason I now know I am so much stronger than I ever was before. I would not want to do it again nor would I not wish it on my worst enemy.

I know one thing for sure I want us to be first and everything else can come after. Alex please do not let me get so carried away with my job that I forget about us please honey I need you so much.

I not only need you I want your body all the time you do wonderful things to me and I love what you do to me. Liz I love what you do to me to I just have always loved you and only you if I had known all these years how you felt about me. I would have had to of made love to you a long time ago. I am so sorry I caused you to lose our baby, and all the pain I caused you. Alex, it was not all your fault. I know it is hard to believe there are so many sick people in this world. This is exactly why I want to do this job so maybe I can make a difference and Alex you can help me in lot of ways you have the experience to make a difference. Alex you know how to investigate these things and these kinds of people. I would love to have you on my team if I can win this thing.

Alex I know the Governor needs to appoint who ever is in the running. I will need you to put in a good word for me. My bosses said they would do the same. I know the State Prosecutor time is up so he is about to leave his appointment so I need all the help I can get. Alex I know you know some of the higher ups and have done work for them. I also know my record speaks for itself. I need is some recognition from the Governor. I know he does not know me from Adam so if you could arrange for and introduction I would appreciate that. Then he could have me investigated and see if my qualifications would be something, they would be interested in for State Prosecutor office.

Alex I know I am asking a lot from you but I really want this job. I think I would be good at it and I would give it my all. Not only for me but also for all the others, that suffered. I know that many of these sick human being's have gotten away with what they do, and I want to stop then in there tracks.

Alex I know this will not be easy but I believe we can make a difference.

Alex this is something you enjoy so why not work to gather, and make a difference. You do not like what is going on any more than I do so what do you say my darling?

Elizabeth of course I love doing investigations this has been my lives work.

Elizabeth I am just concerned about you, I know how much danger you have been in because of me. I do not want to lose you again because of my job putting myself in danger is one thing but I cannot do this to you. Alex listen to me I have come threw all my ordeals with excellence. I would not want to go threw them again but I know God is on my side he kept me safe from deaths door. I think this is something he would want me to do. I cannot go on worrying about my life when I can do so much more than hide myself away. I was not safe in my own apartment and neither were you so there are no guarantees on life right?

I want to do my best to put some of these sick men and women away. I want you with me but if you do not feel right about I will not hold it against you. Alex I love you, and I will respect your wishes. Please tell me that you will try to get a hold of the Governor and see if he will at least look over my qualifications.

That way maybe I can get my foot in the door other wise he will never know who I am and what I can do. Please say you will do this much for me.

Elizabeth I will do what ever I can for you and I will do it gladly. I will help you if you are positive this is what you want knowing that it could be harmful to our health.

Alex as I said our health has no guarantees now does it. No matter what else has happened we have been in danger every time we turn around.

I would feel safer if you and my bodyguard were around me all the time.

Well Alex said he would do what ever he could to help me I knew he would keep his word. I really want him with me in everything I do from now on.

I feel safe when we are to gather, and I like knowing where my husband is.

Alex was busy trying to get an appointment with the Governor. I was caring on with my job at hand making sure the innocent was protected, I love my job but if I think for one minute that my client was guilty or I find they are lying to me I will not be there Lawyer.

I check everything and I have my investigator check everything twice to make sure things is as they say they are. I know that people will lie and try to protect to them selves. I would rather someone tell me the truth in the beginning that way I can sort things out a lot faster.

I have to check out everything to make sure someone tells me the truth. I can protect my client much better knowing right from the start what there story is. I am, known for being an honest lawyer; I pride myself in doing a good job as a lawyer to protect my client. I can be as tough as a bulldog, I am honest I expect the same thing from my clients.

This has been my lifetime ambition to protest the innocent and to see the guilty punished, when or if I get the job as State Prosecutor I will do the same. I will make sure the guilty pays there dept to society. I will feel sorry for those who cross my path I will not have any sympathy for them. I will make sure I will have all my ducks in a row, and I will have everything checked twice.

The time is getting close to when the State Prosecutor time was up, and I have not heard anything from the Governor. I was getting worried if he even was interested in me. Little did I know he was checking out my credentials? I was not sleeping well and I was losing weight? Alex was getting after me about why I am allowing this job to turn me into a skeleton. If this is an indication what this job is going to be doing to you, I really hope you do not get it. I am sorry I just want this so badly, I will do better, and take better care of my self I promise.

The next day I enrolled in a gym to get my muscles worked back up. Then I had an appointment to get a massage and a complete body works, manicure, pedicure, my hair styled. I feel like a new woman Alex was so right I have to take care of my self before I can take of someone else.

Thank God, Alex cares enough to take care of me, and my needs. I told him when we got back to gather to take care of us, and our needs. I do not want our marriage torn apart because of our jobs or anything else. I love Alex, and I want us to work out and to work to gather on and in everything.

While we are waiting news from the Governor, I suggested going to see my oldest brother, and Alex said that is a good idea we should get a way. I suggest at least once a month we take time for us and the family. Alex made the reservations for us, and as soon as I got home from my job on Friday afternoon, Alex had his packing done, and we were ready to roll. He even made sure the dog was in the kennel; I thanked Alex, and told him how happy I was with him. I know life is not easy, for you either honey I want you to know I appreciate you, and love you so much. I really like how you take care of me honey I have never had this from anyone not even my family.

We had so much fun with my brother's family and his three children the littlest one was 1 year old, and she was a real charmer she had Alex eating out of her hands. Elizabeth she reminds me of you when you were a small little girl. You had me wrapped around your little finger and did not even know it. Honey I would have laid down, my life for you. Alex we have made to many mistakes to look back on it from now on lets just look forward, and make our life better.

While we are here, let us just enjoy the good food, and company. My sister in-law was going to have me learn how to bake bread. Well we will see how that turns out I have never made anything from scratch. Alice was so determined I agreed to try. The men were outside working the grill cooking the steaks, and drinking beer and talking. I am sure they are catching up on the past; I know they both have a lot to say to one another after all this time apart. They were the very best of friends while we were growing up. I think it is a shame people do not keep in touch with one another. At times, it is so nice to have someone you can confide in, and trust with your inner most secrets.

When we had, dinner ready the bread baked, and it was not as hard as I had thought it would be. Just time consuming well the real test would be when we had to eat it. The table was set, and the food lay out and it all looked so good. We all fixed the childcare's plate and got them taken care of. Then we sat down to make short work of this very delicious meal. I was shocked the bread actually tasted very good as well as all the other food just seamed to disappear. We sat around the table and discussed the old times and we caught up and to date. I think we should have a big family reunion and picnic so we can be re- acquainted with the rest of our extended family. Elizabeth I think that is a wonderful idea I would love to make the arrangements. Alice you sure after all you do have three little ones to care for? I have plenty of spare time and I can contact everyone to make sure what would fit in to everyone schedule. I will enjoy doing it that way I can see what everyone is up to these days I think it is a shame that we all have lost contact with our very own family members.

Alice you are a very lucky person with you beautiful family. I am so jealous of you and your beautiful children I think you are so fortunate and blessed to have such a great family. I know but look at you a big city Lawyer and wanting to run for State Prosecutor. My God, girl what is up with all of that? Alice I would give it all up for my own family if I could have children. When I lost our baby, I thought I was going to die for sure. I guess God had some other plans for me to fulfill I cannot question God now can I?

Honey you could always adopt there are many children out their needing good parents like yourselves. That could love them and give them the education and loving family life. All I can say is time will tell. Right now, I only have one thing on my mind. I want this job so badly I can taste it and I think I can be good at it. So when you all are saying your prayers at night remember us please.

Alice had me help her tuck in the children then we can all sit around and talk.

When we came into the room, the guys stood up and thanked us for a very good meal. Then we said we could not have done it without you fellows, and thank you for cooking the meat. Now can we have a glass of wine and let us enjoy each other. Well that sounds good to me.

When we were alone Alex said honey I am so proud of you making bread for the first time and it was so good.

Thanks Alex and you were wonderful with them little children they just love you to pieces. I am fortunate to have such a wonderful husband, and handsome to. How much better could it be? I could not ask for a better husband. Moreover, handsome to mercy me I am blessed to have you my wonderful husband. I will not argue with you my dear I am just going to enjoy the time I have with you and thank God for every minute we have to gather. I have wasted far too much time when I could have been with you. I am truly sorry for that I hope some day you can forgive me? Alex I told you there is nothing to forgive we both agreed to do what we did and now that is all water under the bridge so please lets just get on with are lives.

Elizabeth you are the best thing that has ever happened to me. Well then how about coming over here and showing me some of that appreciation big boy.

We needed to get back the next day so Alice had a big breakfast all ready for us. She said we would run you to the airport after breakfast so you can get back to your busy schedule. We sure enjoyed your company it has been way to long lets not wait so long next time. Can we agree to that my family? Yes, we can agree to that so let us not wait so long in between visits.

When we got back to work, I had a big case waiting for me. Not only that I also had a very important looking letter. I said I wonder what this is all about well silly open it and maybe we will find out. I opened it and it said I did not get the job do to inexperience. They had some one else, in mind with a lot more experience then I had.

Well that is that, I tried I guess it is not meant to be. Honey I hope you do not take it too hard I want you to be happy. Please baby will you be all right? Alex I am fine I gave it my best shot and it must not be in the cards for me. I accept that and I know all things work out for the best. I trust God with my life and what will be, will be. He knows our future we do not. This is the way it has to be I am just happy to have you back in my life.

Alex I need you so much we have wasted so much time. I just want us to be happy so we can work on us how about that. Honey that sounds like music to my ears.

We both went to our jobs and did our best to defend the innocent. As time went on, I was feeling very poorly I did not know if I caught, the flu was happening to me Weeks went by, and then months, and I was still sickly, and weak. I looked like a ghost when I looked in the mirror. I was having a hard time with my job it seamed I spent a lot of time in the bathroom. I felt like a rag doll. I had no spine at all I could barley carry my self in the door at night. Alex told me I was going to the Dr. if he has to carry me. I was too weak to argue with him so I let him have his way. I made an appointment I did not have a problem getting an appointment, as my Dr. has been my Dr. as well as our friend for years now. When he saw me, he said what are you doing to your self my God girl.

I am going to run some tests and let us see what we can find out. The next day he called and said he wanted to visit with Alex and my self that very afternoon. I called Alex and told him what Tom had to say. We were on our way to see him and I was pretty worked up I just did not know what to.

Chapter 21

I was making my self even sicker worrying about what he had to say. When we got to his office, they took us, right in and told us to make our self-comfortable. The Dr. is with a patient right now but he will be right with you. When Tom came into the room, he was smiling from ear to ear. Elizabeth and Alex I have good news for the both of you. You are going to be parents Elizabeth you are pregnant, and you need some prenatal vitamins. What Tom that cannot be you all said I could not get pregnant. What is going on here? I am sorry Elizabeth we did not think you could get pregnant after the beating you took. I hope this news makes you both as happy as I thought it would. I am in shock but yes I am so happy Alex can you believe this? Oh, my God honey I am so happy I could just squeeze you to pieces but I will just hug you a real great big hug. Dr. When is this blessed event to take place? I would say right around February oh I am so happy I cannot wait to tell everyone thank you Dr. thank you so much. I did not do a thing you to did all the work. Here is your prescription you get that filled and you will be feeling better in know time. Yes, Dr. we can do that cannot we Alex. We sure can Honey we will stop on our way home. Then I am taking my precious woman to lunch. When we were on our way to the restaurant Alex stopped, and got me a large Bouquet of roses, they were just beautiful thank you honey. What is this for Elizabeth for putting up with me, and for loving me and for having our baby?

Alex I am just so happy I never thought we could get pregnant. After all, they said we could never have a baby after the beating I took. I guess

God has other plans for us and me for one am so thankful. I am happy to Elizabeth I was beginning to believe God had forgotten about us with all the problems we have endured. Well Sweetheart you know what they say? If it does not kill you, it will make you stronger. Well I for one do not like that old saying if that is OK with you? I do not want to be any stronger I would just like a nice pleasant life style like some other folks have. Lizzie will you be quitting your job? No, I want to work right up until I give Birth to our little bundle of joy that way time will go by faster for me. I do not like sitting around twiddling my thumbs I want to stay busy. I think that will be better for our baby to and he or she will be a happy well-rounded and very smart and we will get her or him into one of the best school's around. I want our child to have the best of everything. Elizabeth I want that to but you cannot plan there whole life for them. I know I just want them to be happy I will let them have some in put. All right sweetheart let's celebrate our joyous happy event. Honey I want to start decorating a room for our little one so when our little event arrives we can be ready. I want it to be perfect. Liz it will be if I know you and your family and friends this baby will want for nothing. Alex We need to get registered at one of the best stores in town what shall our theme be? How about Disney world animals that way it will cover all the animals from Disney world like Winnie the poor, Minnie and Mickey Mouse Pluto Alice in Wonderland you know what I mean? I think that is a great idea Alex that sounds wonderful to me. This way it can be for a girl or a boy. After we did all the work on the Baby's room I started worrying what if all our problems we have been going through did not let up. The Baby's life was threatened as ours has been in the past. Alex I know I could not live with that what do you think honey. I believe we do not have to worry about this any longer. I have a new job and most of this was because of me. We live a different lifestyle now you need not worry any more please sweetheart do not do this please.

Alex I cannot help worrying I have been through hell since we have been married. That is damn hard to forget I know what I am talking about and I still hurt mentally and fiscally. I do not think I could handle our baby being punished for our wrong doings. Elizabeth we did nothing wrong we were just doing our job and that put us in harm's way. The sick people of this world do things maliciously and we suffer for doing our job. Now I know that is not right but what this world would be like if there were no one out there putting them where they belong. For there wrong doings have you thought about that and the innocent ones that have paid with there lives for protecting the innocent. How fair is that I ask you now what have you got to say? Alex I know none of this is fair I just worry about us. I have an idea before you get to far along lets take a nice long Vacation. We both deserve that and I think it would make you feel so much better. We need to get a way from all this crime and worrying about things, we cannot control. What do you say honey? Alex I am all for a nice long vacation I have missed so much work already I don't know what the partner's will say to that. Well you will never know if you do not ask right. Alex you are always right I will ask and if they say yes where will we go my darling? Well how about the Bahamas' I hear that it is beautiful there unless you would like to go some where else I am easy my dear so what do you say? I say anywhere you are this is where I want to be. We have been torn apart too much already we need each other now more than ever. I agree so what ever you say that will be it and I will work on the partner's. I want to see if I can get the dog in a kennel before we need to leave. I want to make sure he is well cared of while we are out enjoying our self he is part of our lives to now. I agree my sweet you do what you have to and I will take care of the rest now how will that be? I love you Alex so very much, I love you to my Angel with all my heart and soul right down to them pretty little toes.

Come on now my little worry wart lets make our plans, then when we get back I want to discuss some other plans I have for our little family. Please tell me now I cannot stand secrets honey comes on tell me please. Elizabeth I was looking at this cute cottage with a little stream running right by it. And it has a very large yard with a fence around the back yard. It has a lot of mature tree's and flowers. Elizabeth I fell in love with it when I saw it and I was going to take you for a country drive and just happen up on it to see what you thought about it. I think it is ideal for a new couple with starting a family and all but, it has to be something you like to. Alex I never even had a thought about moving but that is a good idea with the baby and the dog would love it to. I think you have a good idea there I just never thought about moving before. Well I am certainly going to be thinking about this while we are on vacation. I can give you my word on that. Well I certainly cannot' ask much more than that can I. Thanks sweetheart for thinking about it and not just saying no thank you so much. I want to call my parents and tell them about what is going on. Then we can talk some more this evening how that sound does to you my husband?

I will say that sounds just fabulous to me. I will make us some dinner while you talk with your parents that way we can have more time to talk. How about that my little wife? I would love that so much and there are some steaks in the freezer. I will make us a nice salad and a baked potato with sour cream. I have a special thing for our desert. That sounds wonderful honey I am already hungry. I called my parents and I was sharing with them our plans. When I heard another voice in the background I ask who is there? Mother said your Sister just came in the door as you were calling. Oh, Mom I want to come and visit with her to. Well then come on over my dear then we can have a little family reunion. I am so excited I can hardly wait to see her and the family. Alex come on lets go visit with Bernice and the family you remember them don't you? Of course, I do honey so let us go before you have an anxiety attack. I have not seen some of my family for year's. I think I deserve to have some kind of attack do not you.

Sorry Honey I know you are excited but I do not want any harm to come to you or our child so please settle just a little. All right but I am not used to being pregnant this is a new chapter in our book right. I know I have to take it easy, and I will after I get some time with my family.

When we arrived at my parents home Bernice came out running toward us. When she reached me, she hugged me so hard I could not breathe. Oh, honey I have missed you so much and all the while tears were flowing down our cheeks.

Alex you come over here you are part of this family. You always have been and always will be we love you to like a brother.

I know that one that is the problem's Lizzie, and I have had threw the years. That has kept us apart all these years when we could have been to gather. She thought of me as her brother so I thought, I stayed away like a fool. I should have talked to her and been in your lives. So this was my bad and I will never forgive myself for that. I want to change the subject Bernice we are pregnant we are so excited!

I want you to contact me when it happens so I can hear all that spender and love in your voices. Will you do that for me?

Bernice, you need not ask a question like that of course we will call all the family and share our blessed event. Now let us enjoy each other before you have to leave again. How are all the children doing?

Oh, my God you would not believe how fast these kids grow up. Tommy is in High school, and all the other children are in school. I am feeling like all my little one's are flying the coop, and some day I know we will be alone. Until the Grandchildren come, but the way it looks the children will be going to college. I am thinking it will be a long while before they will be having any little ones. I am thinking about going back to work now that all the children are in school. I know that I feel as as if the children do not need me, and Dan is at work all day. I am doing what any red-blooded Mother does when her little flock leaves the nest. I have a good Education and so I am qualified to get a great job as a court stenographer. Well good Bernice, we are happy for you and Dan I presume he is okay with you going back to work? Yes he is we talked about it and discussed it, and he does not see any thing wrong with my going back to work. I think we can start putting money away for building that new home we have always wanted. Oh Bernice I am so happy for you all. We wish you all the very best. I feel like our life is just beginning and you are planning a new life for you and your husband. You are so lucky every thing has always gone so good for you and your family. Liz I know life has been so hard on you. I believe God must have a special plan for you both. You just watch and see what he has planned for you, and your family. I know one day you will call me with some wonderful news I will be waiting. We are to gather so let us enjoy each, and love one another. When a baby is coming, you will not have as much free time, but you both will love it so much. I cannot tell you how much love, and joy you will feel when that new little person arrives.

When it just as well of been wiped out with all the problems, I have had but he gave me strength, and helped me with it all. I have thanked him over and over I know I could not have gone threw it alone. I would not want to do it over again and I am happy that Alex and I have found one another. The Baby is a special blessing for us so I know we have a lot to be thankful for and we are so thankful. At the same time, I am so fearful of what life up a head will hold for us because of our jobs. I could not stand knowing we brought a baby into such a mess.

Honey you cannot think of things like that! Give it all to the Lord and lay it at his feet he can deal with it. Let God show you what he can do, and how strong he is honey he can handle it much better than you or I can. Our God is a strong God tell him all your troubles and leave them with him. This is what he wants you to do he loves it when we trust in him.

All right, I will try what you are telling me. However, why would God let a person be tortured, as I had to endure? I had to kill two human beings to keep my self-safe or to save my own life or my husband's life.

I feel terrible about that and I know God can forgive me. I have ask him to forgive me I cannot help wondering why so many people want to go on killing and torturing and raping innocent people.

Lizzie you know we have a big God scream at him and tell him how you feel. He is a big God and he can handle it scream, yell at him, and tell him all about it.

The next time I was on my knees I pounded the floor and told God just what I was thinking. And how it hurt me knowing that he was to protect us from all harm I feel like he let me down. I am sorry for thinking these negative thought's but this is what I am feeling I need some answer's? I know I need to trust that you know what you are doing. This is very hard for me after I have gone threw all this trouble and after killing someone. I feel so guilty but at the same time, it was he or I. All can say is I am so sorry and I pray I will never have to go threw this kind of trouble again. Now I am never going to think about this again. I am leaving it here at your feet where it belongs. Thank you for listening to my problems I thank you for keeping me safe. Thank you for your many blessings, I love you and praise you I ask this in your name Amen. Now

I am going on with our happiness, and I am going to enjoy carrying our baby.

I love my husband and it is about time we enjoy each other. So far the days have been very pleasant, Alex has been right there for me in every thing I need. I know it had never been very pleasant for us but I am going to learn to enjoy our life and our baby. I now know God has our back and he will never leave us. The Doctor has been happy with me and I have kept my weight down. I have been taking my vitamins, and working every day. I have felt great I have not suffered from morning sickness or any hormonal difficulties. I am in my last month and I cannot wait to see the little one who has been very good baby. We have the nursery all finished and it looks great. We did the baby's room all in pink and blue outlined in white. We thought the baby does not have any certain taste for color anyway. He or she gets a lot older then we will have to re do it to suit them. I have a hard case in front of me tomorrow. I need some one to help me do some investigating. And seeing as to how Alex has helped me in the past I want him to work this out with me. I trust him and I know he can do a good honest job for me. I need this so a man can get a honest and fair trial. I am so big now I have a hard time just getting around in the office and the courtroom. I love my job but being pregnant sure does not make my job any easier. Well Alex sure knows his job because he got all the information I needed this just makes my day now I know I can win my case. Alex I am so proud of you I know you are so talented. I could not win this case if it was not for you thank you so much honey.

Well you come on over here and give me some lip service.

I love you giving me some loving I know you do not much feel like it being you are so pregnant and all. I miss our lovemaking I know this is part of it and all but, I will be glad when this little infant gets here.

I am going to tell him a thing, to about, making me waits until he, or she gets here.

Alex the Dr. said it is all right for us to make love why do you feel like you cannot. I guess I feel like you would not want to, seeing how big you are and all.

Alex I am more than willing I need that more now than ever.

You come here to papa I; want you so much I may not be able to wait on you to be satisfied. If this should happen do not worry I can still take care of you so do not give up on me okay.

Alex that sound wonderful to me I have been wondering what your hold up has been. I just thought I was not appealing to you any more.

Nonsense sweetheart I have always loved you. I have always wanted you so much I cannot tell you but I can show you. Come here you little vixen I want to make mad passionate love to you.

He began by going down to the valley of my body until I cannot stand it I want him inside me. He gently worked his way up to my belly with his tongue not missing a lick. Oh, my God Alex I want you inside me hurry honey. I cannot stand any more please. Mean while he is suckling on my breasts. This almost drives over the edge my body arches with wanting him so. Then his tongue enters into my mouth as he enters into my body I almost lose my mind with wanting him. Alex you drive me crazy as our bodies work feverishly as one then we both cling to gather as he releases his seed into my melting pot of desire. I shudder as I meet his needs as well as mine then we both just cling to gather to enjoy the Ethiopia of our lovemaking then he gently kisses my quivering lips. I am ready once again to have him come in me. I really need this Alex are you ready to ride me again? Sweetheart, I am more than ready then we made wild passionate love once more. As the sweat runs of our bodies, he kisses me ever so sweetly. I pull him in I want him to stay inside me. Alex I still want you can you stand to come again? Honey if this is what you want I am still hard. I will not leave your body until you have been completely satisfied. Then he kisses me with his tongue pondering every inch of my mouth. Alex if you keep this up we may be here all night.

Then he puts his head next to my ear and softly whispers I am ready if you are my sweet. I lay in my husbands arms very well sated I love how he loves me. I know the morning will soon be on its way with its bright and shinning sun and I feel like a new person. Just knowing my husband loves me makes me feel like a new woman. I can accomplish any thing. Well people watch out for what you wish. I thought my world was complete then roof in on me. I got a phone call that sent my world into a whirlwind. Just as I thought, we had it made and all was going right bang right between the eyes. The woman that called me said she had my husband's baby and she said she would like some child support. Well I will talk with my husband and then we will see what his story is. Give me your number and I will have him call you. I was so upset by the time I entered our home I was just shaking in my boots. I need to hear Alex part on this story before I pass judgment on him. When he entered the house I was waiting for him with baited breath. I said I received a fascinating phone call today. Alex said yes and who called? I said a woman said she had your child and she wants child support. I do not know what he will say but I need to hear his side of this.

Well that is possible but I will need a paternity test before I pay any thing to any one.

Liz, you were married as well so do not condemn me for being a man. I am no saint and we were not to gather at the time I had an affair. I will take care of this matter and see what is up with this woman if the child is mine I will take care of it.

I never in my wildest dreams thought about Alex being with another woman. I do not know what I expected of him but not this I always thought of him as all mine. That is crazy I know but this was my thought I felt very devastated. I feel as though some one hit me in the stomach and knocked the air out of me. I was having hard time breathing, and I was getting sharp pains in my stomach. It was so severe it was causing me to bend over with each pain. I said I think our baby has chosen to come into this world right now. I need to get to the hospital get my bag in the closet. About that time I felt like I had wet myself and it went all over the floor and me. I could not help myself it just kept coming and oh, what a puddle it made. After we got to the Hospital, they took me into a delivery room, and gave me a shot in the arm. When I woke up, I looked at the nurse and asked her when am I going to have my baby?

Honey you already had a bouncing baby boy with all kinds of black hair and big blue eyes. He is doing just fine your husband is with him now we will bring him right in to you. Were you planning on breastfeeding him? I certainly am I want him to feel close to his parents and to know we love him. When they brought him in to me, I was awestruck with some kind of awesome wonder. H e looked up at me as if he knew me. I smiled down at him and I just started crying. I could not help myself I hugged him up to my face and kissed him. You look just like your daddy thank you God for this little baby boy, and for him being so beautiful and healthy. The tears just kept coming I had no control over them it was as if the dam broke. All the water in me was overflowing. Alex he is so perfect I cannot help my self,

I know honey and I want to thank you for a good job you have done. The nurse came in and said would you like to see if he would nurse you? I am ready I pulled up my gown and put my breast in his mouth and he latched right on. I said I think you must have taken lessons from your father you are doing a good job. The nurse said well I do not believe you need my help and she left the room.

Alex came over kissed me, and said honey I am so sorry this mess showed up now this should be a special time for us.

Alex this is our time, and I will not let anything ruin it. I love our little one so much, and I love you for giving him to me. I reached up, and kissed him and told him how much I loved him.

About that time he said what are, we going to name this little monkey. How about Adam Jerome that sounds good to me I do not even get an argument out of you.

Sorry I am too happy to argue with you. You win all the time any way so I will not waste my time. Honey I am leaving you for a while but I will be right back okay? As long as you do not lose your way that will be fine, we will miss you. Alex came over and kissed me hungrily with all the love he had for us was right there in his eyes. I fell asleep and when I woke up, I was expecting my husband to be there. He must have been, delayed or some thing held him up. I knew he would be here soon so I drifted back to sleep. The next thing I hear is the nurse waking me up. I said is it time for the baby to nurse? She said no I have some bad news for you oh my God is something wrong with my baby? No but your husband has been in a car wreck. He is in pretty bad shape they have him in surgery now. As soon as he comes out I will come and get you so you can see him. It seemed as it took forever I took care of Adam he was such a good baby. I really thought the hours were dragging by I repeatedly called the nurse's They answered the same all the time we will come and get you as soon as we hear anything all right? Please I am so sorry, but I am so worried I cannot stand not knowing what is going on with him. As time was going on very slowly, I started walking the hallways. Then I went to the baby ward so I could look at the baby. I needed something to hang on to while I had to wait. I knocked on the window to get the nurse's attention please bring me my baby I need him now please. I tell you what you go back to your room and I will bring him to you. I was rocking Adam when the nurse came into my room and told me my husband was out of surgery. Oh good could you call the nurse to come and take the baby back to the nursery. I want to be with my husband. When we entered the room I was so surprised I could barley recognize him his face bandaged to his eyes.

The Dr. came in to explain what happened to him. He said Alex had a broken jaw, his nose was just hanging there so we had to do some plastic surgery. He had some broken ribs, and internal injuries. and a lung that was deflated. He has a broken shoulder and a cracked pelvic so he is going to be here a while.

Alex I am so sorry this had to happen to you. Please try hard to get better we need you my darling. I am to afraid to touch you I know you are hurting. I am here for you I know this is not going to be easy but we can get threw this. I am praying for you every second of the day. Mean while the people from my office has been drifting in and out of the hospital. They have been bringing gifts for the baby they are such nice gifts. I said thanks to all of you for your thoughtfulness, and the flowers have been beautiful.

Well Liz you deserve this and more to you and Alex have been threw so much to gather. We will keep you all in our prayers, if you need a baby sitter so you can visit with Alex please call. My Mother and all my family have been calling to see how everything is going. They said please keep us up on how Alex is doing and we are happy the baby is doing so good. Remember we love you and Alex and the new little one take care of your little family.

We will be praying for you all, and remember we love you, and Alex so much. After 24 hours were up Alex took a turn for the worse.

The Doctor said he had caught, and infection and in his weakened state it is not good. After a few days Alex did not recover his strength he just got worse.

They called me into his room, and said spend, as much time with him as you can he does not have much time left. I could not believe my handsome strong man could go down hill so fast. A week went by, and Alex was like a skeleton. He did not make it threw the night and he was gone. Then I had to deal with his funeral, and the insurance co. was suing the driver of the other car that hit Alex. I did not know if I was coming or going my head was throbbing. I called my Mother and told her I need you Mom. I cannot seem to get my head wrapped around this mess do you know what I mean?

Honey I cannot say I know because we have been so blessed. I cannot imagine all you have gone threw, and you are still sane. I will do what ever you need me to do I am here for you sweetheart.

I broke down and sobbed my heart out Mom what am I going to do know? Alex is gone, and I have a new baby to bring up by my self.

Honey I will do what ever you need me to do. I will do it please you can count on your Father and me. We will babysit for you whenever. You and the baby can move in with us. That way while you are at work you will not have to worry about the baby. I think that will be the best all around for you and the baby what do you think?

Mom I will think about that okay right now we need to plan a funeral for my husband.

The funeral went along nicely a lot of Alex friends showed up and showed there appreciation. The people from my office showed up and some I did not know. The luncheon after was very hard, and having to speak to all these people was especially tough. All I wanted to do was curl up in a corner and cry.

Everyone was so nice and wished baby and I well, and offered up there condolence's.

Then there was Evelyn she showed up with her daughter in tow and shouting so all could hear her. I want you to know I do not care if this son a bitch is dead. I am going to get are share of his money and do not be mistaken about that.

The usher's took her outside, and what happened after I do not know. I knew she would not go away so, I had to get my head on straight.

Mom I am going to take you up on the offer to move in with you, and Dad. I am going to have to put my head around this problem as soon as I get back to work. I am so happy that Alex was a donor so all his body parts went to some deserving people. Well little Adam I guess it is you, and me big boy. For now, I have to get this woman off our backs. Adam just kept nursing, as he never had a care in the world. I kissed his little hand, and pushed his hair back off his head. I cannot believe we created this little bundle of joy. Alex, I have loved you so long I do not know how I can quit now. Oh, Adam I hope you can hold all the love that I have for you. I am going to have to love you for both of us. I am going to have to be Mommy and Daddy to you. You will never understand how hard it has been for Daddy and me. Life can throw you some awful curve balls. I hope I can protect you and shelter you from all of that. However, son you will have to go threw some hard times to just as we have had to do. Maybe you will not make any mistakes or have to go threw anything like we have and that is my prayers for you. I wish no one person would have to go threw some of the things we have had to go threw. I love you my sweet handsome man I put him on my shoulder to burp him. And it did not take him long he was such a good baby I cannot complain at all. I am really going to miss you little man when mommy has to go back to work. I hope you do not give Grandma a bad time come here my little man. I pulled him up to my face and kissed him all around his little mouth. He acted like a little bird wanting something to eat. I guess you are still hungry all right come on you can have some more to eat. I put my breast in his mouth and he ate as if he was starving. Well you certainly eat like your father he loved mommies breast's to. Then the tears began again they just rolled down my cheeks like a waterfall unchecked. I cannot believe I still have enough water in me to keep up with all the tears. Lord, I am so thankful for this little man. I do not know what the future holds for him, and me but we have gotten this far. So we are going to trust you are here with us and you will never leave us in our time of need. I am giving you my son to protect, and guide him, and to love him as I love him. I cannot give you any thing more precious than this. You already have my love and my man so this is all I can give you. I have nothing more! Well I went back to work; after I used the breast pump to get enough milk for my little man, I sure will miss feeding him. I do have an hour for lunch so I will go home and feed him. Mom will make sure not to feed him until I get home. That way I will not be leaking so badly. Things were going so good at work and home we all were so happy. I do not like looking a gift horse in the mouth so I will just enjoy it while I can. Low and behold, just as we were all snug as a bug in the rug boom lightening hit yet again. In the form of my last husband that had given me so much trouble. The devil he Donald had been released from prison and wanted to see me. I just cannot believe he would dare come near me again after all the problems we had. He was saying that he had gotten angry management control and he had changed a lot I know I was so controlling and jealous of you. However, can we just be friends, I will do what ever you want me to do. I just want a chance please I need the work, and I am sure we can work to gather as a team please. I beg this of you if I get out of line you can get rid of me. I was so skeptical, and afraid of him, and I had to think of my son as well as my self. I do not want to leave him Mother - less. I want you to continue in your anger management classes and if you fail to go, I will have your consul or call me. Do you understand me? I am not going to play around with you, I hurt by you once, and it will not happen again. I have a baby to take care of, I will not put his life in danger. This will only be a work related relationship. I do not want to see you around my home what so ever. I will call you when I need your service's. I went home to discussed this with my parents my Mother, was the first to express her opinion. Oh, honey I do not know why you would want this man in your life again. Well Mother he is a very good Investigator. I do need someone to investigate before I take my cases to court. I really do not trust him either but I fell as if I should give him an opportunity to show me how much he has changed. I have his consultant's number so I can check on him all the time and they will call me if he fails to show up for his classes. I promise to keep close tabs on him at all times if he screws up even once that will be the finish of him. I can't allow any one to hurt my child, He is my life. Well do not say I was not against this because I don't like it one bit. All right mom I just wanted your opinion not a lecture okay. If he ever shows up here, he will be dead. I will personally shoot him. You had better let him know how we feel about that. As I got back to work one of my colleague has met me half way down the corridor. What is up?

They said I have this big case and I was wondering if you would be interested in it. If so, it could bring you a big promotion. Not alone the money is very good and I know things have not been too good for you lately. So what do you say to this offer?

I will be happy to handle this case.

I just want you to know it is not going to be an easy one. If you cannot handle it just let us know. If I take it I will handle it, since when have I not handled a case? I just want you to know how important this case is. This one is our biggest clients and this is a big chance for you to climb the corporate ladder. Well thank you for thinking of me, I truly appreciate everything you do for me. I went into the office to meet with the client and I could not breathe. This man was so handsome I forgot to breathe. Then I heard someone say Elizabeth are you all right. I finally came to my senses and said excuse me for being so foolish. I was lost in my own thoughts there for a while. Can you ever forgive me? I sure can you are such a beautiful little thing I can forgive you anything. Well thank you but you are just too kind. And what may we help you with? First, and foremost of all my name is Greg Harrison Jr. I am sure you have heard of me.

Well I am sorry but I am just getting back from a medical leave so no. Sir, I do not know who you are or where you came from. Now I am sorry, but you can have the privilege of filling me in on whom you are and what you stand for. Now may I take you out for a drink so we can get to know one another? What is your story that we can be of some help. You know my name is Elizabeth so will you join me? I was having a hard time trying to keep my attention on business. This man was out of this world drop dead handsome. I just could not see myself working with this man. I am having trouble breathing as well as keeping my mind on what I was supposed to be doing. Greg I am having a problem with you so would you mind postponing this meeting until tomorrow. Well if you would not mind telling me, what the problem is maybe I can help you? I am having a problem keeping my attention on the subject. I have to many things on my mind right now. Come now Ms. Elizabeth tell old Mr. Greg what is really bothering you. Well Mr. Greg it is your attitude you think by snapping your fingers everyone will just buckle down and worship you. I am so far ahead of you right now. I knows how you think because you are so handsome you can have what ever you want. Well not me sir I am not for sale at the bargain table. I will work with you on a strictly business bases. So if this is fine with you lets get on with it if not I will say goodnight right now. Okay we can do this your way. I do not want to get into any kind of relationship at moment anyway. Well would you like to tell me why you need my service, my service is expensive and I am paid by the hour.

Well I need you because they think I killed my wife.

Well did you kill her and tell me the truth. If I ever find that you are lying to me about one little thing I will be out of here so fast it will make your head spin. I called Don and told him I had a case for him. I needed to talk to him could I come over to his place?

He said sure I will put on the coffee pot. I made it over to his place in no time and knocked on his door. When he opened the door, I could see he was not alone. Don this is strict information I cannot have all you friends knowing what is going on. With my cases, you know this is strictly private between my clients and me. I have to trust you or we cannot do business do you understand me Don?

Do not worry so much honey I have always kept everything between you and me confidential have I not?

Here is the person I need you to check on keep it on the qt. This man is a very important person. I need this information as soon as possible. If you do not want the work let me know right now. Elizabeth what the hell is up with you? I just want to be sure of you and that I can trust you? If you ever betray me, you will be the sorriest man this side of the border. I will have you up on charges so quick you will not have time to blink. Why are you doing this to me? I have never let you down on any of your cases before. So why are you being so tough on me now? I am sorry Don I guess I am feeling insecure about myself. It did not take Don long, and he had all the information I needed to go to court. The State Attorney had filed for the court date. I called Mr. Harrison and informed him that we will show up for court. Greg said he knew it already. Well I will see you then in the mean time stay out of trouble. I mean if that is possible what are you trying to say I always stay out of trouble. That cannot be true or you would not need a lawyer. Well I just wanted to meet you so I did my best and here we are. That is nice of you but please do not do me any more favors. Then I hung up the phone I wanted to spend as much time with my son as possible. I laid him on the bed, and lotion ends him down from his little head to his cute little toes. Then I put his clothes on him. I was talking and smiling at him he smiled back at me, so cute. I proceeded to baby talk in his language. He was talking gibberish so I did the same thing to him he acted as if he understood me. I blowed air - bubbles on his little tummy and he laughed right out loud. I love you my little man I miss your daddy I wish your daddy were here to watch you grow up. We waited for you so long then when we get you then they take him away from us. We will have to believe God knows what he is doing. I will do my best with the help of your Grandparents to raise you in a good honest God fearing home. I know I will not be here a lot of the time. Your Grandparents will be here for you when Mommy is working. I am so sorry that your mommy has to leave you but you will be safe. Just you remember Mommy and Daddy will always love you. All right now little man we are going to take you out for a stroller ride. This way Mommy can get some fresh air as well as some much-needed exercise. I was enjoying looking at the neighborhood lawns and flowers. It was such a beautiful day the sun was shinning and it was so warm, I felt like God had touched my life and took away all the hurt that my life and body had gone threw. I felt like a new person from the inside out. I said a prayer and thanked God for every thing he has done for me. I stopped in the park, and sat down, picked up my precious son, and thanked God for him. I love you my little man. I was giving him a ride on my leg making him go up and down. He was laughing and having so much fun. I just could not believe we could have so much fun together doing nothing. Come here my sweet little boy I snuggled his neck with my mouth and kissed him. He just laughed, and laid back for me to kiss him some more. I could do this all day, I put the blanket down on the grass and changed his diaper and got out his baby food. I wanted to feed him and let him take a nap. I would eat a sandwich and have some fruit and a drink. While he slept I was reading a book when I heard some one say it is a nice day right? I looked up and there was Mr. Harrison, and what would you be doing here in the park on such a nice day may I ask?

The same as you my dear, spending some quality time with my daughter.

I did not realize you had any children! I am very surprised I just never pictured you with a child.

Well she is right over there playing in the sand with one of her friends. She has made friends with her since we have been coming here. What is her name? Melissa Ann that is such a pretty name,

You certainly do not hear it that often.

Thanks, may I ask, what is your baby's name?

Adam Jerome well now that is a name to grow into I certainly am optimistic for him. I know he can have or make anything of his life. With the Grace of God and good parent's and Grandparent's to help him I know he can have it all.

You are certainly sure of him are you not?

Yes I am there is know reason that he cannot make it and be someone great. No matter what it is he decides to do he will always be great to us.

I know what you mean, they are always great in our eyes no matter what they decide. Parents always think there child is perfect right?

Know truer words were ever spoken my friend.

Well I think my daughter is ready to go home. Well sweeties are you tired.

Yes, daddy my friend had to go home, there was no one to play with. I want to go home now daddy: come on let us go.

Well Elizabeth, I will be waiting to hear from you with some good news. Then just like that, they were gone as quickly as they came. Little

Adam was such a good boy he slept all the while I was talking with Mr. Harrison. I wanted to finish reading my book while Adam slept and hope that I would not have any more interruptions. Then with out fail the baby woke up probably wanting fed and diapered. All right sweetheart I will take care of my little one. I fed him first, and waited with the diaper change until he finished eating. Well now with all of that taken care of I think we should go home young man what do you think. When we got home Mother was waiting for us on the front porch. I said hi mom is everything okay. She said sure is now that my 2 favorite people are home safe and sound. I know I should not worry but that is what mothers do.

I just hate that you need to worry about us Mom, but I do understand. Mother did I tell you if I can win this case it means a big promotion for me.

Well dear, I will pray about that to night when I am saying my prayer's. Thanks mom for praying for us, I really need God on my side. I have to do some studying tonight can you take care of your Grandson please? While I was looking over the papers Don gave me, I was a little overly excited about what I was seeing in black and white. I said to myself if this is right then Greg could not have killed his wife. I called Don and said hey Don is this everything that you have found on Mr. Harrison?

I have a few more files here, I will bring them over tomorrow at your office if that is okay with you?

That will be just great; I will see you tomorrow then.

When I reached my office, building there was Donald waiting for me.

Here I brought these files for you; I am sorry I am so early but I am going on a fishing trip. I just want to get an early start. Well you should have said, so last night, I could have come over to your place and picked them up.

That is all right I have everything so now all I have to do is get there. Well then good luck, I hope you catch many fish.

Thanks, I hope so to well I hope these papers will be of some help for you and Mr. Harrison.

I would say they are going to be a great help! Thanks it is so nice to know I can count on you again. You really are a great detective, and you are honest and, I know you will always have my back. Thanks so much, and I will be taking care of you to. I will be putting a check in the mail today will that be satisfactory. Liz you know I am not worried about that so whenever is quite all right with me. Well then, I will be seeing you and good fishing. When I reached my office door, I noticed some one sitting in my chair.

I ask my secretary who is in my office.

She said Mr. Harrison was waiting for you for about an hour. Well I guess I will have to see what is on his mind. I entered my office and said hello Mr. Harrison, I hear I have been keeping you waiting?

That is quite all right, I am so anxious to hear what is going on with my case. I am having trouble sleeping wondering what is going on.

Do you have any more leads, please do not, keep anything from me please?

Well Mr. Harrison I would have contacted you today anyway. Yes, I have some good news for you and as soon as I get myself situated, I will try to explain it to you.

Can I be of some help in getting you situated? Alternatively, shall I just sit here and be quiet?

That would be nice if possible. I need some time, to get this straightened out and get some coffee in me maybe then I can explain it to you. Then my secretary brought in the coffee I thanked her and she left the room now may I offer you a cup or something else to drink?

Yes, thank you that would be just great.

Now if you will let me get this sorted out, I will explain it to you. Thanks and then he sat back in his seat and waited on me. When I finished I looked him right in the eyes, and said well Mr. Harrison we have a good case. I believe we can win this thing hands, down so if you are ready; we are going to court.

H e jumped right up out of his seat and was around my desk in a heartbeat, and grabbed me and put a lip lock on me like; I never been kissed like that my whole life. I thought I was going to faint, I brushed my self off and sat down at my desk and took in a big breath, and gave off a loud sigh.

Well now, can you give me some information or is it a big deep secret?

I Think I can share some of it with you and do not get your hopes up to high we still have a way to go. I know my dear I can remain cool as long as I know we have a chance.

Well everything is checking out so I think we have a good chance. So now, we just have to wait for a court date, and for us to pick a good jury. I am warning you right now do not do any thing stupid.

What do you mean by that statement?

You know very well what I mean do not go trying to bribe a jury member, and do not talk about this case with any one. We do not need this to be broadcasted, and in the paper's or on the television or radio. I do not want you tried and hung before we can go to court so please keep a low profile.

Yes madam I will be a good little boy.

Thank you I will appreciate that very much.

Now go home and spend time with your lovely Daughter.

I would like to spend some time with you my lovely beauty.

That would not be possible we need this kept professional no hanky - panky sir you know that.

I need to keep my head on straight and try like hell to get this case dropped, or to find you innocent of any wrong doing'.

Well when this is over I am going to be all over you and you will not stand a chance against me.

You will be mine, heart, and, soul, and body. I want you for my wife so you think about that while we are waiting.

Every day with out haste, I received flowers at the same time every day. I could not believe how many flowers he would send, and a note with such sweet sentiment. I tried to keep my head on straight but it was so hard with him doing all this mushy stuff. I know he was priming me so I would be ready and waiting with open arms when this ordeal would be over. I have to dismiss all of this from my mind and keep it on my case. Well with the information Don had received we won the case now this door is closed.

Then another one would be opening up and I knew Greg would be looking for an answer. I really had to search my heart for this one. I was afraid of making another mistake.

I need to see you please say you will come with me to night.

I agreed when he came to pick me up he was being chauffeured in his limousine.

He came up to the door and handed me a bunch of red roses for you beautiful.

Well thank you sir I really appreciate this just give me one moment to put these into water. I am ready sir.

Come on Elizabeth you can do better than that we have been threw a lot to gather.

When we entered into the limo, he put his big strong arms around me and planted a big kiss on me.

I could not breathe or think then he kissed me again I feel as if I had died and gone to heaven, and I did not want to come back down to earth.

Elizabeth, I have wanted to do this for so long. Sitting next to you, everyday in court was painful when all I wanted to do is grab you and make love to you.

Oh Greg I could feel all that and more then he kissed me a deep and lingering kiss oh Greg my Darling what am I to do with you?

Elizabeth just say you will marry me and make me the happiest man on this planet.

Greg yes, I will Marry you I cannot stand this any longer so I will be happy to marry you.

Oh, my darling you have just made me the happiest man on earth.

Greg you have to know one thing I will not tolerate anyone mistreating my son or telling me what I can or cannot do, I want the freedom to make up my own mind.

That is just fine with me darling we will get a nanny for him if you wish.

I have no idea right now: I will think about this.

Come here my sweet then he kissed me as his hands roamed up my blouse as he latched on to one of my breasts, I said I am sorry but my baby is nursing me.

Good Then he will need to share with me is that okay?

All I could say is go for it and oh, my God, he was making me so hot, I could hardly stand it. Oh, Greg I cannot stand this please quit.

Not now my sweet you are mine, and I want every bit of you now. Then his hands were in my panties pulling them off as he entered himself in to my throbbing wetness. He was fully erect and very large, as he pumped himself into me and we both came at the same time. I almost forgot what that felt like and oh my God, it has been to long. I want a lot of that honey.

All I could say is oh yes me to me to, well Greg and I have been married for 2 years now and it has been perfect he is a good Father to his Daughter and my son and we will be having a little one around Christmas time. We are so happy and by the way, our baby will be a little boy. Greg is happy to know there will be a boy to carry on his name.

Written by Carol J. Aken